ROOM
LITTLE
DARKER

June Caldwell worked for
many years as a journalist
before becoming a writer
of fiction. She has an MA
in Creative Writing from
Queen's University Belfast,
and lives in Dublin.

ROOM
LITTLE
DARKER
JUNE CALDWELL

NEW ISLAND

APOLLO

an imprint of Head of Zeus

First published in 2017 by New Island Books
Published by Apollo, an imprint of Head of Zeus, in 2018

9 7 5 3 1 2 4 6 8

A catalogue record for this book is available from the British Library

ISBN (HB): 9781788542883
ISBN (PB): 9781788542906
ISBN (E): 9781788542876

Typeset by JVR Creative India
Printed and bound in Germany by CPI Books GmbH

Head of Zeus Ltd
First Floor East
5–8 Hardwick Street
London EC1R 4RG

WWW.HEADOFZEUS.COM

For Adrian Caldwell

Contents

Upcycle: an account of some strange happenings on Botanic Road

LIVE BORDERS

It is hardly worth telling, this story of mine, or at least in a modern context, because so many people go through the same these days and feel it too dull and inconsequential to mention. We have to take our modern horrors on the chin in the same way sewage is turned back into drinking water, axiomatically. Some small trace evidence of evil was always there, hanging on a hammock off his organs, in the grubby suitcase inside his head: laughing at a rape on the television, laughing at the old woman up the road dying of cancer (in the most excruciating way). Laughing at a crushed dog out on the main road, a cut knee, house repossessions, floods, poverty, puberty, forest fires, riots, stock collapse and all else sitting mean and keen in-between. Dead in my head now, lost to me, lost to the ignorant beauty of everything.

There are days when I crumple on the couch giving in to endless interlude, boom-box of Jeremy Kyle, mini flask of vodka, crows crying their lamps out in the chest-hair back garden. Slow Joe next door moving his furniture around to nothing but his own sound. Eventually I'll squirm up to bed when I know I've successfully folded enough hours of the day into the next so that neither is in much of a shape to be useful. Even then I cannot escape the watching. That his eyes are stuck on me and me alone, I am completely sure. That she is unable or unwelcome to come through at all, I am also completely sure. From his hospital bed he seemingly figured it all out. 'Here ye go Frank, have some nice yoghurt, c'mon now, try to eat a little something …' The mind is a peculiar thing, the nursing manager told us. He seemed to know we were doing up some of the rooms, I told her, he said so. He said he could see it in his mind's eye. 'That's impossible,' she replied. 'He might've heard one of the carers talking about renovating a house or something along those lines. If you think of it a bit like the way magpies work … on clear days when the blood flows normally, they snatch bits and bobs of other people's reality, processing it as their own.'

I always had a strange relationship with this house. When I left for university in London twenty-five years ago, I was plagued with memories of levitating in the sitting room as a small child. When I returned to Dublin on holidays my mother wrote it off, sniggering – oh my daft daughter! – but he didn't. 'I used to do that in digs years ago, down the quays,' he told me. Levitate after concentrating like mad. Best done standing upright with your fists clenched by your side, head up, breathing deep. Think your way through the weight of human rubbish, out the lid on the other side, slowly ascending. Think yourself into light-footed, sheer, insubstantial. 'If you lose confidence even for a second, that's you,' he explained. 'You'd be right back on dry land again. Sometimes it might only be an inch or two you'd go but what of it. Other times you could go high into a dusty corner of the room no bother.' One night after his roommate caught him the 'old bag' who ran the boarding house called in a priest to ceremoniously bash and threaten with stern words. The priest, when he realised my father was a mossback atheist, called in a mutton-faced Guard and the Guard called in a Doctor of Psychology after he demanded to know what the exact charge was. In 1950s Ireland it was put down to a physical malaise caused by communist blathering. They backed off with a polite warning. He was a civil servant by then; that particular type tended to get away with a lot.

My brother Arnold, six years older than me, remembers *Top of the Pops* posters falling from the four walls in the back bedroom when he stared into the old grotty dressing table mirror. The same dressing table that recently got an upcycle by Annie Sloan chalk paint that transforms any surface without the need for undercoats and such. Myself and a teenage pal Geraldine used to sit drinking cider and smoking dope in that mirror until she eventually got the creeps sufficient and wouldn't come to our house anymore. Another brother, Paul, went clear mad in that room. Ran off to the British Army and got caught up in the Falklands – not actually fighting

– but overseeing penguins and derelict army buildings when everyone else scarpered. He put a £90,000 bet on a horse and flung himself out a B&B window in Warwick after they paid to get rid of him. My mother invited him home to rest it out but he stayed five years and turned mustard yellow in the room. He eventually died giving himself over to numerous medical trials to feed his gambling habit. He always said he saw faces and not just in the dead leg of night. Mean wizened women's faces, out of holy nowhere, in the glass panel of the kitchen door leading out into the back garden. There were so many rumours about the clump of houses (not just ours) not far from the old walls of the Botanic Gardens in Glasnevin. In Irish: *Glas Naíon*, meaning 'stream of the infants'. A stream infected with famine-time cholera from sinking bodies in the nearby crater of graveyard. That was one theory for some residents going a bit plinky-plonky. Ley lines, lead pipes, electrical brain teasers from mobile phone masts. Nothing was ever proven.

It was a sky-drenched night in November sometime in the late 1970s when Frank came home with chicken balls from the Chinese. He was pissed out of his brains as usual. From the crimped lace curtains draped across the sitting room window I saw him crawl on his blue-gout hands and gabardine knees from the Datsun Sunny, unable to walk upright on two legs. The takeaway stuck to his teeth like a Residents' Association Annual Dinner doggy bag. There'd been rumpus of a dog with rabies scaring women and children outside Our Lady of Dolours Church. Aulones hen-huddling around

laminated posters of a neon thermometer advertising
the advantages of the Billings Method for holy contraception, paying attention to the sensations of sacred
vulvas. They talked about the rabid dog with juice spilling from his mouth. At age nine, I thought the dog might
be Frank. He was so very angry every evening when
he returned home from work. Arnold was in the porch,
mop of blonde milling into his young punk girlfriend's
face. 'Get that slag out of here!' Frank roared, as the key
hunted the bockety lock of the main door, crooked on
its cheap wood frame from previous assaults. A favourite
trick was to catch one of the sons just as they reached
freedom point, banging the growing body he owned up
against the glass panels, shouting, 'Think you're able to
get out of here easily buster!' I scurried from the sitting
room into the cloakroom in the hall, shutting the door
tight, lighting my magic candle. The whiff of sulphur
from the match a strange comfort. A scuttle of some sort,
then a very loud scream. My mother and sister's voices
snaking the air in high venomous pitches. Oh a clump
then. Body falling with a thump and thwack. Slush-
puppy red blood on the wall, as I'd soon see, being wiped
with small yellow sponges by small white hands. Paul's
head split open with a car jack. 'Go to bed!' my mother
screamed. 'All of you, get to bed, I'll deal with this.'

Point is, he was never going to leave the house willingly, even in ancient age. And the house was never
going to spew him up willingly either. In reality he had
this vulgar indwelling of power despite the whiskey having pinched his mind, his heart, his intellectual abilities,
his ambition, his bowels, his bank, his false teeth, his

legs. When they first married my mother Emma was his World War II coal queen for sure. The newly built 1950s semi-D had four fireplaces, including one in a double bedroom upstairs for any wife to squeeze babies out in comfort to lay snug in a chest of drawers. No one bought cots in advance then. A mantelpiece adorned with a Padre Pio genuflection, ceramic Holy Mary, broken fire-guard, a photograph of her dead father dancing at a tea party and a Dusty Bin; won in a Blackpool bingo hall in 1981. I was born in this room.

Back in the days of pat-a-cake, of hand-jive, when asked that first time she curbed a smile, and ran like mad, in her A-line skirt and Bobby-socks. My father ran after her. All of what you'd expect, naturally. It may have been the dead baby, lifeless in a Clarks' shoe box on the bedroom floor, that had the final say. Or it may have been nothing peculiar at all. Missed promotion in work, boredom, a stray urge. But sometime in his thirties, he left himself and us behind. Yet we continued to love him despite the emotional violence, the daily drudge, the drinking, the incessant arguing, the drab awful iron-clad impossibility of it all. As you'd expect towards a father or a husband by a certain societal proxy. A hangover from Victorian times, maybe. We loved him because it was required of us. We battled hard to understand why he was always in such intense pain, why he needed to pass on some of that pain so readily to us.

For the last three years, with everyone else gone, he'd wandered into the smelly elderly and utterly struggling pit. Manning the walls all day like a woodturner. Agonising over what we now know were mites of madness softening at the base of his brainstem. He cried out in the Murano glass corridors of sleep and at least a few times a night would clamber into our bedroom, where my mother and I slept after he became properly incontinent. Cumin-coloured puddles on the brown lino in the bathroom, all the way down to the extension where he sometimes relieved himself in a green bucket with a broken lid if he got lost. He'd enquire as to where he was, looking for an explanation for the clatter trap in his head. Kept saying 'sorry' for something he was never able to remember having done. 'I can't cope with him anymore,' my mum said. He had dementia. We were exhausted. It seemed no one else out there cared. Our local GP said he no longer made house calls because the HSE wouldn't pay doctors for such variants of care since the recession. He had to make it to the surgery or rot. Towards the end of two summers ago, maybe in 2013 or thereabouts (it's hard to recall exactly), I rang social workers attached to the local health board, put a plan in place and that was that. We were not to know what would happen. We had no experience of this kind of thing. Even in retelling the story, I find I'm just as upset and confused as when I lived through it. I cannot be absolutely sure of what occurred, of the timeline, except for the following: the day came. We both said, 'Be strong, this is it, the only way forward!' Even as he sat in his wheelchair facing out at the eggy sun for the first time in four years, the house showed signs of a problem. A water tank in the attic, only replaced the previous year, decided to manifest a swollen belly on the toilet ceiling, bursting through its own guts before the lift arrived. A mirror smashed with no window open or air circulating anywhere. The fridge gasped itself to a halt. I looked right at her and said, 'Don't even say it! Don't be ridiculous! Don't be reductive! We're doing the right thing.' I felt that the whole point of being here, of being human, was to take responsibility. That's what we were doing, surely? God knows he couldn't do it. He was incapable of *doing* anything. 'Try to remember that much,' I said to mum. She suffered hugely through all of this. She had made her bed. She would 'till Doomsday' lie on it.

Four days in a row he rang pleading for his life. We told him 'NO!' He could stay there for a month and give us time to clean up the house. It smelt like a Berlin urinal. It would have to be fumigated for starters. We would have to organise a new bed. Possibly a downstairs toilet with washing facilities. There might even be a grant available to convert the garage as elections were only around the corner. 'I can't cope with this awful place, you're my wife, please take me home!' My mother never stood up to him, ever. She tried to poison his stew once, but that was a long time ago. Rummaging around the garage shelves for the black and yellow box. Me in my brown school uniform, cradling her from behind as she stood at the bubbling pot on the free-standing gas cooker caked with dirt, tipping it in like a schitzy witch. 'You're in there for respite. I need a rest too,' she told Frank, slamming the phone down. On Day Three he had a bombastic stroke. On Day Seven we were summoned. 'He has deteriorated significantly, especially emotionally,' the nurse said. 'I'm so sorry, but it could've happened anytime, anywhere.' We didn't quite know what she meant by that but when we saw him, by Jove we got a shock for sure. We'd traipsed the ward three times before we accepted the sack of crumpled grey maudlin was the same feisty person we left off just the week before. It took three more days and threats of legal action to get him moved from the stinking old TB sanatorium in the park to a proper hospital for the specialist treatment he needed. *Do Not Resuscitate*, the sign above the bed read. Young slip of a thing from Killiney or somewhere affluent like that said with his age, with his expected quality of life, with the general prognosis (of which they were still not fully certain) there was no point in doing much at all. Just sit it out, wait it out. His life was now a junk shop egg timer. Throat broken. Stomach empty. His head, well, basically in not so many words, it had begun to thoroughly scoff itself. Middle cerebral artery: considerable shrinkage. Clots: many. Brain bleeds: more to be expected. Aspiration pneumonia. Muscle damage. He screamed. Roared. Pegged at us as if he were grabbing on to a half-inflated lifeboat. We should go home and take it handy, try to get on with things. Especially her, his wife, the overseer of his decline. She needed to push ahead, look after herself. Put loose things in perspective. Everyone will get to this point. There's really little to do when it happens.

That night I woke at 2.23 a.m. I will never forget the exact time because I saw in the pitiful light of the green alarm clock, my father crawling around the wall like a crazed lizard. His body partially flattened with his old navy office clothes flipping and sagging. A much smaller head, but his eyes: a ferocious sickly yellow. His neck bent as if it had been snapped and yanked back into place with a heap of loose skin sewn back on roughly. Flipping and flopping around on top of the Billy bookcases, side to side, like you'd expect to see in the House of Reptiles at Dublin Zoo. The most revolting noise as well. A kind of clacking that didn't befit his human form. His smaller body thumped along the furniture as if he/it wanted to attack, priming itself for incursion. I sat up and rubbed my eyes. Flicked on the bedside lamp. Checked for my mother in the other bed to see if she was still in deep snooze. Her small frame slowly rising and falling back into the pink sheets. I was stuck in the forecourt of some outlandish car wash, with the engine on and no idea where to head to next. I stayed like that for a good hour and the vision of absolute repugnance didn't falter or fade or go away. I could barely breathe or move, my limbs became sore with fright. I could hear the mechanism in my chest chug out and suck in stale air, but I carried on watching him flip and hurtle and scoot with no sign of halting. Until that bilious moment in time I thought I knew what being on the planet entailed, what it was all about, what I could expect at the worst corners of paranoia or down times. But I knew nothing. It had become rayless in a sore nocturnal second; opaque, obscure.

Just once, a bitsy time in autumn 1982, did he catch hold of the ethereal air balloon and partially rise to the skies. It had been another dreadful week in the house, the first coal fire of late September. In the kitchen we'd placed blue diner chairs around the roasty flickers, toasting slices of Brennan's bread on long meat forks at the very top of the fire. My sister Lucy started a new job as medical secretary in Doctor Steevens' Hospital and was home early. Frank was on one of his extended rampages, resuming yesterday's argument with whoever he could as soon as he demolished through the door, carrying it on into tomorrow, leading back into today. The rule of thumb was to stay still and silent when the key clicked. To see. To see if the coat would be thrown off and deposited at the end of the banisters. If he couldn't be bothered to walk to the cloakroom and hang it up, it meant business. He banged through to the kitchen and said, 'Well?' Of course no one answered. If you answered it would be a dragnet. 'Well, anyone got anything to say? Anyone feeling brave in here?' We did not answer. He bungled past the side of the Formica table, banging into our lovely fireside chairs. He seemingly jumped high in the air (no one dared have eyes on him to see it happening), landing on Lucy's bare feet with his chunky brogues. Of course she wailed, as you'd expect. Paul, who was hiding behind the fridge playing house detective, two years older than Lucy, ran out and grabbed Frank by the shirt collar, dragging him out to the hall backwards as he continued to wriggle like a Mekong giant catfish balancing against the top ridges of a too-small boat. Paul bounced on him, kicking him in the full of the back and head. So many tunks and clonks. 'Kill him!' Arnold shouted. 'Fuck him up.' I milled out into the back garden and stayed there until it grew dark. I shadowed wild pigs and razor-tusked beasts with a makeshift spear one of the boys stole from a day out at the Scouts, fashioned from a sweeping brush. It stuck in the grass at brilliant primitive angles though it took some skill to get it to stay rigid in the mud of the vegetable patches. It seemed the rest of them forgot about me or else they thought it was best I stayed lost out there for a while. When I rambled into the sitting room some hours later after it got too cold, Frank was collapsed unconscious on his armchair that no one else was ever allowed sit on. 'Don't look,' my mum said. 'Look straight at the telly, here, you can hire it if you like, just this once.' She handed me the huge remote control boasting eleven fat buttons. Such a rare treat, especially as it was brand new, snugly wrapped in a thin film of moon-blue plastic.

After the lizard sighting my mum claimed she'd heard him calling out for hours, Emma! Emma! Emma! 'I'm not the better for it,' she declared, the next morning. I was up at the crack of dawn trying to steady myself, doing things around the house that had been abandoned for some time. 'It's understandable,' I assured her. 'It's a kind of guilt, you know, you're feeling all out of sorts with the way he is, what he's going through.' No, she was utterly convinced it was really his bellow she heard. 'At one point I even heard him knocking on the window trying to get in.' I thought of their window, the front double bedroom window, climbing out when we had the silly séance with a matchbox as a planchette back in the day. We all legged it from the house in unison, a herd of eleven-year-olds. 'Move if there's anyone here! Move if you can hear us!' Then it flew off the bed, hitting the radiator all the way over at the far wall. It seemed an impossible manoeuvre for one of us with our little fingers and no experience yet of the trickery out there in the vast sickly world. Vickie Cawley laughing as ten crows.

Me in pure fright mode. Billie Dunne jumping out that bloody window twenty feet up and running for dear life. It was only two weeks after she found the baby in the plastic bag down the laneway backing onto the Sisters of Our Lady of Charity convent. Same location where they later found twenty-two babies and sixty skeletons of women whose deaths were never registered. Billie stumbled across the bag in 1981, opening it up without really understanding what she was looking at. Though a tiny bloodless hand was enough to send her rocketing. I guess this was how young women got rid of unwanted evidence back then. It wouldn't happen now with advances in DNA, with advances in social conscience. On the day of our séance my mother was working at the RDS Horse Fair on the Rowntree's chocolate stall: Munchies, Caramacs, Mars Bars. All the leftovers were piled into a large shopping bag and dragged across the city home to us. It was the first time I was allowed look after the house without Arnold or my sister Lucy in situ. When my mother got home, she slapped me clear across the chops. She may have already met one of the mothers on her way – Billie Dunne's was particularly hysterical – but if not her trademark intuition told her I had got involved with something unenlightened. Something mischievous and corrupt. She could feel it. The cold throughout the house was cave-like, wet and heavy.

The next visit wasn't even in the deferential cubbyhole of night. I was sitting on the toilet with the door wide open, staring out into the landing, thinking. It was mid afternoon. Thinking of how to make her life better in the time she had left (she was already eighty years old). Thinking about how to access his funds to do essential repairs to the house, especially the kitchen and damp bedroom walls, which were, after years of neglect, in a dreadful state. Everything was in his name. She was Mistress of Nothing. What I saw next makes me feel like I may have already been a composed and submissive inmate in the Asylum. He thundered up the stairs his head intact as I had remembered it but a spider's absurd blackened body, eight legs quivering on the carpet in front of me. Darted about turning to stare me right in the face. In a moment's stampede of panic he was gone again. I jumped so quick off the toilet screaming at the top of my lungs, 'Mum! Mum! Jesus Christ, help me Mum!' Back to being a child again.

There was this thing about seeing Frank on stairwells. Around 1986, I was a teenage Mod with a sharply carved Bob, blue bootleg trousers, a round puppyfat face slathered in Rimmel pale-biscuit make-up. I worked the summer months hand-delivering invoices around Dublin city for a pinstripe freak who sold encyclopaedias to people who wanted to show off knowledge on the shelf. Life was good, I was toying with freedom, heading to all-night Northern Soul dances and live music gigs, new people, new sensations. I lived on a diet of space dust and cans of Campbell's meatballs in gravy. The quays were full of antique shops, musty solicitors' offices and telephone boxes good for drinking on the hoof when the 7 p.m. witching hour hit. I spotted Frank on my postal rounds early one afternoon climbing up a metal staircase on Ormond Quay fixing his trousers, fixing himself, zipping his life back up. He seemed properly smug and satisfied. Smiling minus that trademark sneer. I honestly hadn't seen that before, Frank as haphazard man. He stared at me and I at him and we both walked on by without a word. 'He won't last like this,' my mum said when I told her. 'He can't go on.' She was fairly sure she could get him back on track if he just knocked the booze on the head for a few months or more. He'd already been with her friend by then too and in the pitch of night she'd stay up around the smouldering ashes to write him letters her doctor advised would help. She was to make sure to throw them in the fire when her emotions were done. It wouldn't be fair to expect a man like that to take on all manner of female fragmentary. He had a very important and utterly stressful day job that many men of lesser stock couldn't endure. That night, after I'd seen him in town on the black basement steps, he returned home with Chinese chicken balls once again, this time for the whole family. Lava-hot balls of scrumptiousness in mini grease-proof bags, snowed in gorgeous lumpy rock salt. When you bit into them the chicken played a strange trick on your tongue, opening out like a new expensive umbrella, pushing suitcases of hot batter around the gum-line. For a few hours, it made us ridiculously happy.

Of course my mother was no longer capable of remembering these golden nuggets. All this harping on about how the stroke was probably our fault. We didn't give it to him! If he just allowed a bit more of our help at home, we would not have insisted he be removed in the way that he was. Obviously he had a problem with it too. What we needed to know was if he was doing this deliberately. Was he wilfully, determinedly, trying to teach us a lesson for what we had done, when in reality, we were left with no choice by then? 'Dealing with this is like dealing with a forest fire,' nurse Bláthnaid said. 'Even people with the height of expertise cannot deal with this at home sufficiently. There comes a time when you have to let the person go.' He is talking about old relations long-dead and I asked her, 'Could he really be seeing them?' It is a 'thing' with people who are sick, apparently. He will not be aware that they have already passed. Is he caught in some foyer between? I wondered. 'It doesn't make sense that he would ask about his brother Edward,' my mother said. 'God knows he couldn't stand him when he was alive. Him or his ugly Sligo wife.' We have to stop this, I told her, we have to accept that he's getting the proper care and we have a right to live in the house now, the best we can. The kitchen had been fixed up: cream shaker with high-quality Italian stone tiles; a new water tank with titanium coating; floorboards in the front bedroom replaced entirely (as the urine had burnt right through). 'For a second I thought he was there in the porch late one night,' she said. No! That was the milkman I told her. At this stage it helped to be stern about the whole ordeal. Such was her slave mentality towards him for so long that she found it almost impossible to disentangle from him in any meaningful way. We painted the bedroom at the back where we both slept a genial grey, with some of the furniture a Provence green to ward off the evil eye. The garage was cleared of his things and the garden tidied up to such an extent that you could now sit on a small stone chantry down the end and draw in the air in long protracted puffs.

At evening time I thought it best to summon him in the mirror to stop any of the nonsense that would no doubt occur later on. She was already so scared of going to bed that I moved her into the spare single room where he wouldn't think to go. All the years growing up he never bothered any of us in there. I gave her some Ambien along with a few Panadol to aid sleep into the night and sprinkled some valerian and Roman Chamomile essential oils on her pillow. Tucked away in there from early evening until well into the following day, I began to feel that she was not part of this anymore, that I had chaperoned her away from potential suffering or fright.

His presence in the dressing table mirror was amorphous and vague, as if to show his full self to me was not part of the greater plan, that I was somehow not worthy. He would not have been like this with any of my brothers, had they been alive, but men of his generation were sodden in misogyny whether they cared to admit to it or not. Though I didn't doubt for a second that he was there, looking back at me, sneering, informing me that no man would come to the door in a rush to take me out, that my skin wasn't the best, that really I wasn't the cleverest of them, a few forks short of a picnic basket, and more besides. His seething hatred began to make me laugh, as if any empathy I had left for him and his lousy condition was hidden away in a beanpole storage facility, the type that people use for bundles of clothes they hope will come back into fashion someday. 'Do you think I don't remember what happened on Bingo Nights all those years ago?' I told him. 'When I pissed the bed and you rolled me out like a sausage roll and said I had to wait in the hall until Mum got home.' Putting me in that whiskey-fart bed on Sunday evenings because you were too lazy to babysit properly downstairs, when all I wanted was to watch *Worzel Gummidge*. What a lousy father you were but still you made us feel sorry for you. It was always about you. And what the hell did you do for your parents after they left Ireland? You barely bothered your arse ever seeing them again. When you did you were pissed out of your mind. They rang us here to complain, across the Irish Sea, you with no respect, turning up for funerals two days late. You who demands so much of us now! What a bloody joke! Do your worst, go on, do your worst. Do whatever you think will work at this stage and do it with your sick brain in all its shrinking glory! Oh but if you think it stopped him slinking into those horrible animal forms and darting around furniture at night, my grousing in the mirror only made him worse and brought him nearer to me, instead of up on top of the bookshelves or the wardrobes or the wall. A ferret slinking in and out of the bed bars at my feet, leaving drops of sweat and other depositions for me to see in the mornings.

When she passed away in the single room I didn't have her removed straight away because that's exactly what he would've *expected* to happen. He'd expect her to be lying there, in state, in Massey's on the Old Finglas Road, a twin set and her navy skirt (always in navy, like a sailor's wife on a first trip abroad, hoping to appear smart no matter where they would go). I didn't mention to him either that she was gone as I wanted to see if he'd tell me about it, if he really had the upper hand when it came to using his intuition, his greedy appetite for a good hunch. But he hadn't a breeze! He did however begin to appear more frequently, more sonorously if you like, in the mirror. I am not sure if this was a kind of latent protest, but the house joined in by breaking even more of itself up. The heating system gave out and the plumbing at the back of the shower fell to pieces completely. Twice I had to get a local hood in to bash things back into place or replace the piping entirely. Black mould broke out on the walls of both bedrooms. Dreadful shapes in butterfly splats and distant familiar outlines (the one of the Eiffel tower was funny, but I made sure not to laugh out loud), which I'd rouge over with the Annie Sloan chalk paint within hours of appearing.

I miss her terribly but part of me is glad she is resting up accordingly. No more, 'Oh God, do you think we should go back out to him today? Does he have enough dark chocolate? Is there still a problem with his swallow? Are there enough clothes out there? I don't want them to think we're not making enough of an effort.' She had herself tortured to the point where she gave Catholic martyr wives a pitiful name. Sad too that she would never get to go on a Royal Caribbean Cruise ship that I had promised we'd do. Those ships are something else! Ascend three hundred feet above sea level in a North Star capsule! Fine-dining extravaganza that holds more than two thousand merry-makers at a time! He hardly took her anywhere truth be told, not for a long time. Hadn't the energy, or the self-governance.

Now that it's just the two of us I feel I have an opportunity to understand him a bit more. I hope that if he sees that I know how he feels, how hurt he is, he might stop his games around the house and reach some sort of compromise. The dressing table was made for them when they first got married by a very talented carpenter, huge money, with the promise that no other identical piece existed in the whole of Glasnevin. The mirror carved in a classic baroque style. It's good to concentrate on the positive aspects of where we were now, and to forget all the things that didn't work in the past. He wanted to be a writer, for instance, but couldn't quite stick at it, not like I am now. 'There is a lot more to life than jumping at every silly ambition that lands on your mat,' I told him. He thinks this is a sound observation and one that will ward off disappointment from expectations that are perhaps a bit too high. 'That's the problem these days, people want so bloody much,' he says. Isn't it so true! We are able to agree, which I feel is genuine progress. To think we were so petrified of him all those years ago when he was the one who was clearly so terrified of us. I get that now. Christ do I get it. That I would hide up here under the scratchy horse blankets during fights. Fingers so deep in my ears they'd be sticky and sore when my sister would eventually burst into the room to reef them out again. 'He's gone off to bed,' she'd say. 'The coast is clear for now and Mum has yummy shortbread in the oven.'

Leitrim Flip

I would never tell a hound like that I'd done it on purpose. You can't predict the 'switch' and though he seemed more cuddly-do than spanky-don't, the army background was a clincher. It was also the only time that I'd get to test him properly in all this, the juncture where I cradled the dynamism, not him. Oh he hadn't managed to keep his eyes open wide enough at all. Like most men, he'd stupidly underestimated me. I dumped him before we'd begun to see how he'd jerk and crawl. He texted back quite surprised with a simplistic 'I understand'. I hadn't expected that smack of humanity, it made me feel contrite, for a nanosecond. Then I considered he may have done it on purpose to achieve the desired effect, to manipulate. He was a Dom after all. It was the first day we'd met in person. He'd be discarded hours later

for being a mindless superficial twat. And a hypocrite.
I couldn't stomach a man inside me who hadn't the
ability to think things through beyond the half-baked
one-dimensional. *Stick your fucking brain in me first before
you stick your cock in!* Truth is, I wanted to see how he'd
react given that he'd be playing me like this in my role
as a sub into the near future. I wanted to witness how
he'd jump, psychologically. It's hard to find people on
those kinky websites who'd go the whole hog. I was
also just out of a long-term relationship and I felt like
fucking men over big time. Could I bear being back in
that grimy white work van of his horsing through the
streets of Dublin with my huge tits bobbing and the
lyricism of his voice swinging around his Adam's apple
like a Satanic hammock? 'You think so slave, can I stop
you there, have you any idea what you're whittling on
about, are you totally clueless, have you any notion of
the world you've stepped into?' Mouth mouth mouth.
He really didn't shut the fuck up. There was hilarity in
it too, but a lot of latent aggression for sure. The wanker
thought he was so smart. An ex-Marine no less. All that
vicious training, all that PTSD, all that crying alone in
stone bathrooms in foreign places with too much sand.

When we got to the hotel room he was anything
but smart, flying around in a Dickensian mania (Mr
Bumblefuck). He had his gut unselfconsciously splayed in
full view and his leather play kit glory-holing itself on
the dressing table where the slick menus and tourist bumf
usually sit. The words were farting from his ginger gob,
doing a very good bluebottle impression he was, buzzing
to the bathroom, then back out again – 'Oh, see, I like you

slave, you're just my type' – circling the bed with a creepy half-smile, back to the bathroom again, talking like a pirate turkey stuffed with amphetamines. Then the runny shite came, endless diarrhoea sentences as he tried to get a grip on what he was actually doing. Was he capable of squirming into the dark at all? Though as I'd soon learn, the one thing he could do without having to concert-direct himself with hot air was tie me up. To tie my hands behind my back shrewdly and roughly (and even then he lost the key, still stuck in the handcuff, the gobshite!) and there I was with his fat cock in my mouth hurting my jawbone. My carefully applied whore-red lipstick smudging all over this stranger's pasty skin, the idea of having to chomp on it interminably until he shot a bad-diet-load down my gullet. To be totally fair it was a nice sensation being restricted in movement with his warm flesh in my gob like that, a first for me. I felt properly submissive in this moment. Up down up down slurp slurp all around trying to use my mouth to piston and position him so I could make him 'orgasm'. He was enjoying that I couldn't quite manage it, laughing at me, chortling, so cheap to do that but I understood the effortless humiliation in it for him. Two-pissholes-in-the-snow blindfold cemented on which meant I genuinely couldn't see a damn thing. Not one of those sex shop synthetic pieces of crap but a proper patch-per-eye medieval yoke which he'd bound very tight. My arms were really hurting yanked behind like that; I hadn't bothered telling him I had back problems caused by the fucked-up hips and afterwards of course he'd blame the fat. A brute like him doesn't wait around for explanation. 'You nearly had me there slave but you let it go!' he announced. 'Fuck's sake I almost came!' As if I was supposed to read his twitches like a basket of braille bundled by the cottage fire. I moaned loud for him to remove the cuffs from behind my back. My tits were preventing me from grabbing his cock and working it with my hands and tongue simultaneously so we could get out of this kip he'd booked and pour some pints down us like he'd promised. When he released me I grabbed hold of him like a boat part I'd no interest in but had to rough-house to get on with the boating holiday regardless. 'You nearly had me there again, fuck's sake slave get a move on!' I wondered how much the sound of his own voice could stop him from coming. Even his cock must be totally sick of hearing him. I imagined him at home fighting at the dinner table with his Debenhams-clad wife. She'd be good-looking enough given that he's a big ego. Good-looking in the conventional sense of looking OK in a swimsuit for her age, but a head like a horse, with too much make-up splattered all over. I could imagine him swinging the breeze not letting her away with a stray consonant during arguments. Sitting room bully. Bedroom bulldozer. The only way she'd be able to get her own back would be to stop fucking him, which is probably why he was here with me. He'd be one of those slow-release tormentors who could be sappy when convention required (important calendar dates: anniversaries, Valentine's Day, Mother's Day). His need for control a driving force both blinding him and shoving him forward.

He came then, suddenly, with a screamy shudder. A small spurt of what tasted like leftover sweet 'n' sour from a drunken weekend's Chinese takeaway. His balls were properly deflated, hanging like empty sacks of rice. Thank God that bit was over. He pulled me up and unbuckled the blindfold. Sunlight pissed all over me. He'd no interest in throwing me over the bed and riding me hard which he'd been threatening to do on email for days. No, it was now all about him and the pursuit of city centre hooch. Can't even remember if he bothered to use the crop or flogger on me at that stage, despite my heavy hints by coyly mauling his trade tools through my fingertips every time I tiptoed by where they rested, redundant. There was just one crafty moment where I felt he had more power than me; when he grabbed my hair unexpectedly from behind and flung me down on the bed. The weight of his physicality pinning me there, face scraped in the cheap cotton of the over-washed duvet, the feel of his harsh breath behind me, the strength of his arms. I wanted to shout, 'Keep going soldier boy, keep going!' but he was too interested in getting out into a shite pub up around Camden Street somewhere. I'd see more of his masterly skill later, but for now it rested pretty in his emails where he'd write sexy shit like, 'Next time slave, I'm going to introduce you to subspace, it's about time you became acquainted.' That excited me. I'd read a lot about it. Seemed wholly technical, like a Master or a Sir would need proficiency and artistry to get you there. To empty tingly endorphins into your system via the fever-burn of the whip. Taking you to a megalopolis of filthy sensation beyond the blandness of a naff hotel room. Beyond where you'd ever thought of going on your tod. A euphoric place only a pervert could perfectly locate on the mind map. 'You'll be tied to the door frame,' he informed me. 'You'll dance to the music as the crop sings. You'll be whipped all over too, hard. I've never met a cheekier submissive. I'll bring ear defenders, the type we used on the ranges. There'll be no safe word allowed for punishments. Be prepared slave, you will not be able to sit for a week.' I'd asked how he knew when a sub reached this fabled place. 'When she stops dancing,' he said. 'When she's no longer able to wriggle at all.' Jesus, that turned me on. The manky idea of total compliance. Unhooking me from the straps fastened to the top of the door after I'd stopped twisting and flailing, dropping me into his big animal arms; that first embarrassing tinge of intimacy. Though for now he was still a stupid wanker with no idea he'd be dumped in the morning as a display of *my* power. Instead of saying 'do you want to play soldier boy, then let's fucking curtain-raise for real', I turned to him when he asked was I ready to vamoose and softly replied, 'Yes Master, I'm ready.'

In a cage in a kitchen in a farmhouse in Leitrim. Master pacing the ground with hairy belly hanging. Bog all room. Caught for days on end. Hours fleecing hours. 'Grab that fucking bag slave, if I push your arse right up to the bars, stretch your arms out, grab the bastarding thing, pull the handles in, slide it over, from under that chair there, I've a taser in the bag, I'll do the bastards.' Then what? We're still locked in a cage, with the pair of them pleasantly electrocuted and still no fucking escape. 'Your fault, this,' he says, crawling over my legs, bashing against my hips. 'Fuck's sake give me some room!' Master is always prepared for these things, what with being a soldier. Except he's not. 'It wasn't my idea to meet up with them,' I remind him. The husband feeding us from Pedigree Chum bowls while the wife saunters in and out in a pink babydoll chemise filming on her smartphone every half hour or so. Jewelry, watches, bags, coats, play kit, shoes, underwear, taken, gone, confiscated. Ceiling cameras scattered around. Streaming a live feed to a website. Fuck knows what pervs are watching. Twice a day the husband enters in a leather gimp mask, fully concealed, raining down with rivets. Brass padlock on the mouthpiece. 'Nommm nommm,' he says. Wearing nothing but a harness with mickey pouch. Bull whip in hand. Lashes the cage bars, long noisy cracks. Grunts through his gag. The wife laughs; sweet chuckle of a librarian who's stumbled across a chalky first edition and can't help but wet her knickers. 'Be good doggies now,' she says. 'And there'll be special treats later.' Makes husband a Cup-a-Soup. Mushroom. I am ravenous. The smell is intoxicating. We squash to the very back where the patio door is. Husband moves to whip the sides. Eventually the tip of the whip reaches our skin inside. 'Fuck's sake, I'll knock your block off as soon as I get out of here, I'll shit in your wife's eyes, I'll snap her legs, pull one off, beat you with it.' Master needs to calm. It just makes them laugh all the more. He keeps winking at the husband like they're both supposed to know something. 'Can you put some briquettes in the range?' I ask, I plead, I stare at the wife, I beg. 'It's freezing cold in here, please.'

She looks pissed off. 'That's no way to address me,' she says. 'How should I address you?' Master hands me the laminated instruction sheet from yesterday, or the day before? Address Kennel Owners As Follows: 2 'woofs' for a request, 3 for the litter tray, 2 small whimpers for a toy, full bark for collar and leash ...' It goes on. 'Woof woof,' I say. Master pulls the back of my hair, knocking me to the ground from the hind legs position.

George's Street, Dublin, on a steely Friday night in citrine taxi light when we get together again after the first hotel meet. 'You have to taste the guacamole in this place, it's like nothing I've ever put my filthy tongue on. They use whole lime skins and whatever way they mash it all up, it's phantasmagoric ...' Big words irk him. He's wearing a fat priest black polo neck and some shite corduroy pants (couldn't call them trousers). 'I don't want no poncy place slave, all that nouveau cuisine bollix, give me steak and chips, that's me sorted.' We ramble through the heavy door and I immediately nab a waiter to secure us two stools at the bar for the next hour and a half. You can't book a table in this place; I knew that'd be nothing but botheration for Master. The only other restaurant we'd been to before, he complained like fuck from the off: the cramped table top; the lack of hot spice; the tepid temperature of the curry. Commanded me to the toilet so he could bellyache without the presence of a weak-minded woman looking on. 'It better be good slave, this is your city, not mine.' I recommended the Taco Laguna: stir-fried Iberico pork with summer vegetables in a lettuce cup. I thought it might appeal to his virile carnivore.

I loved the music in this place, clatter of eighties tunes on a loop, banging loud. 'A lettuce cup, are they having a fucking laugh?' There were twelve 'rules' he'd given me and only two I abided by. 'I'm not shaving "from the neck down" to be hairless. It's ridiculous, way too much effort, especially if I only see you twice a month,' I said. 'Have you any idea how long it takes to shave a snatch totally bald? It's worse than plucking a Christmas turkey. Housewives gave up that shit in the seventies when supermarkets spun modern.' I ordered the Roast Gambas: Pico de Gallo, guacamole and crema queso in a taco shell. He wasn't impressed at the €17 price tag. 'Are you going to pay for this slave?' Well, given that he was the self-confessed Commandant in Charge, I assumed he'd get the bill. 'You're not wearing the collar either, did you think I hadn't noticed?' I refused to wear the thick worn-leather neckband with the cattle ring on the front. It was vile. Dog-like. Or worse. Bison-like. Or worse. I wanted a decent sterling silver band, discreet, not particularly noticeable. 'Don't you get this? You do as you're told slave. You leave all the decisions to me, you obediently follow instructions, ALL of them.' My boyfriend, The Narcissist, only recently walked. I missed him like mad even though we hadn't humped for three years and all was rotten in our State of Denmark. I used to munch here with him, holding hands under the table, superfluity of life plans over frozen margaritas. We'd buy a small cottage in Stoneybatter when my parents snuffed it. Get the attic converted into a double sleeping platform with a ladder so his kids could stay. Tile the backyard, fling it with plants. Pay the €5k for a gorgeous white wood burner in the sitting room. He'd be sickened at this new inroad. He'd want to protect me from noxious kink. 'This is not you love. You're way too sensitive for this shit.' Ah but I'm not. Didn't we learn so much about our repressed selves by that traumatic parting? 'I feel so mentally crazed so much of the time, I just want someone to take me in hand, to show me how to behave,' I'd tell him. 'You know? Not take any crap, knock some of the meanness out of me I feel with the pressure at home.' His navy eyes, his lovely face, his endless love that died like a pig. 'Ask one of those prats for some napkins slave, this tack is runny as fuck.' On Master goes. 'See those cheeky messages you send me on KIK all the time telling me that I'm a deadhead from a rubbish high-rise in Glasgow who can only spell phonetically, I hope your arse is able to cash the cheque for that?' I'd already explained I was an 'alpha submissive', a different hybrid to the pain sluts and gormless kneelers. 'That first night we met,' he says. 'We got pissed and you dumped me. You do know you're going to have to be severely punished for that?' They stroll in two seconds later, pre-arranged: Malcolm and Sarah from Leitrim. Master shakes the husband's hand, kisses her sloppily on the cheek. 'Game on,' he says, all happy out. She scoops up the last of the tortilla chips, lathering them in precious guacamole. Tall and slim. He's tall and creepy. Twenty minutes later we're on our way to Leitrim in a white Hiace. Out on wide roads where growers set up spud stalls as soon as the bad weather kicks in. Maris Pipers, Roosters, Queens. 'You're pretty,' the wife says. 'Big porno boobs.' Thistles scratch the car windows too fast. In the retina of a running rabbit there's an ache for warmth but it'll never arrive. 'You're nice too,' I say, not knowing what I'm really supposed to elucidate back. Two and a half hours later we arrive at a dirt track too lurid to be a boreen. The house sits on its own scrubland with an abandoned boat stuck on its side filled with compost. No lights. No neighbours. No salvation.

Saturday or Sunday in early glow as Lord Canine and Mrs Mutt are nowhere. Certain moments are elementary, so simple they become eternal. Photons of electromagnetic radiation travel forty-five billion years to reach earth and we're still only at the stage where microwave ovens are modern. With these moments of clarity we learn to value tiny things … chronology makes everything solid and strong. That's what I'm telling myself. We're fuck all on the grand scale. Master has only recently (within the last few weeks) admitted it has all gone very wrong. Intended as a coaching exercise on compliance for me. His stomach is deflated. There are large sores on his legs; hag's faces painted in dangerous red. When I look at them I remember the first satsuma I scoffed in school in 1974, digging my fingernails into the scabrous skin, smelling and tasting the miniscule bursts that shot out onto my chin. He's not speaking much. I too have lost weight, but am feeling hopeful. During the day I take turns crouching on each bum cheek, still plump enough to supply some cushion at least. If I press up against the front of the bars I can stretch my legs partially lengthways the full width. Up out and over the cluttered window pane full of dusty toby jugs, the honeysuckle French kisses the sunlight, bowing to our subjugation.

Panicles of whorled branches, purplish-brown, prised open, spreading in fruit. Tufted grass with creeping rhizomes. I've never felt happier scoring the different colours in the sky, diffracted through the air. Here, a field of phantom cattle clump about joylessly scaring the *púca* that once leapt on a local man's back. We were given a handbook of local legends as our only reading material. The man, who is forever nameless, managed to stab the entity with a penknife and throw it to the ground. When he returned the following day he found a wooden log with a knife-sized hole along one side. 'What was it like fighting in the Falklands?' I ask Master. He doesn't answer straight away. The only avenue of punishment left. 'There was logic to it,' he replies. He hasn't taken the beatings well, sobbing for hours, refusing to communicate or look at me. Squashed into the furthest corner, throwing up some gobbledygook at an absent wife. 'When I get back I'll get the gas boiler serviced love, I'm sorry I've been away so long.' Unlike me, when I reach the puddle of tears, no longer feeling a thing – when Lord Canine uses the really thick rattan cane – it purges every bristle of stress, setting me up for the whole of the next day. Our bodies are deeply marked in thick purple stripes. Skin on my thighs broken open a number of times. Pain so excessive and profound, I pass out cold.

In they saunter with a group of five rubber gimps. One doused in duck yellow from head to toe. His rotund vacuum-packed belly and peaked hat a delight in a way. Master whimpers dejectedly. 'Here are our precious doggies!' Mrs Mutt says, pulling out wooden chairs to form a neat row for the spectators to get comfortable.

I immediately fall on all fours, turning fast in manic circles so they can see the butt plug with fawn fur tail wagging devotedly. 'Woof woof woof woof!' I say. I've perfected a deep meaningful growl that represents not aggression but cute little playing sounds to please my owners abundantly. 'Isn't she a joy!' one of them in a black and white Victorian maid outfit declares. 'Totally smashing!' says another in a gas mask. God knows what rural hills and crannies they slipped down from for a few lost hours. If they've emerged from the stinking steam of packed dairy sheds or if they've run out of Rosewood French doors in architecturally designed contemporary bungalows facing strategically southwards. 'What breed is she?' someone else asks. Master flings me a stingy look, very like the first time I climbed into his van and he told me to prepare for a journey like no other. 'She's a Dandy Dinmont Terrier, cheerful nature. He's the opposite, Golden Retriever we'd great hopes for, but he won't even mount her anymore.' Lord Canine piles stray wood into the range. His fetish flippers smacking the ground as he carefully plops about. 'Are the bold doggies hungry? Do the bold doggies want some succulent strips of beef? Have the bold doggies done pee pees on the floor?' I leap up and tear at the first piece of overcooked meat flung, licking the residue of grease pearls dripping down the fortified steel billets. It's twenty years since I've eaten animal flesh but endurance has taught me to accept every small gift graciously. We're no longer fed from bowls since Master began attacking in rabid fits. Mealtimes triggering his prey drive. As if deep in his medulla oblongata he knows to bite a human moving too quickly. I hear his stomach rumbling like distant thunder muttering imperfectly from the purl of clouds. It's unlikely I'll be able to date a normal bloke after all this is over. I've thought about this a lot. Sitting in a heaving sports bar in Dame Street all faux giddy when Manchester United score a goal. All that droll macho nonsense. When escape comes, whether in three months, eight or a year, I will recall all these particulars. 'We're never getting out,' Master says. I'm shocked his army training hasn't served him in more callous or mercenary ways. He really is a depressed moron. 'It can't be that far to the N4,' I've told him, numerous fucking times. 'Remember we only beetled off the main road for a few kilometres to get here.' Even if it was a miserable day with flea fogs of rain obstructing vision in every direction … when our cage is being cleaned and one of them makes the systematic error of turning away for a microsecond, we'd bolt. Once, Master grabbed me by the throat when I described this very scenario, banging my head so hard Mrs Mutt tore in from the sitting room hurling hot tea at his snout causing incalculable torment. 'Whoever picks us up on the main road eventually will hear us yelping like we've never been able to yelp before.' Master bangs his rump against the padlock to get attention.

All five stand up in a splodge of vibrant PVC blushes, making their way to the bars so the rest of the room is concealed from our view. They bend over us, all whoop and holler, pulling at the cage so it tips slightly. We topple about as if inside ferry kennels on top deck on a stormy day. I know exactly what to do. I fling myself on my back and open my legs wide. Two paws scrunched up over clamped breasts, head hanging to the side for a champion view. With the temperature rising I begin to pant heavily, sweating like mad. I make it achingly clear for Master there's only one option left to cool me down, to cool us all down. It rests solely with him now to do his thing and get enough oxygenated blood back into this ecosystem. I pant even more to seal the deal. After it's over we'll curl tightly together, snuggling into well-deserved sleep. Free to run at breakneck speed along the most beautiful sweep of beach. Tearing up lumpy dips of sand so relentlessly our tails stop wagging and our legs collapse under the weight of yummy ecstasy. Running, scampering, sprinting, until nothing we've ever been through before matters.

Dubstopia

Scrambled egg beside a steaming gee-pad Carol left on the mattress. Lidl brownie with ants. Two empty packs of Amber Leaf. Wet jeans. Sun tearing in the window through an A-line skirt she stole from yellow teeth Bag-Face in Oxfam. Book of Yeats's poetry open on a fumble in a greasy till and add the halfpence to the pence. Leather Joe's address book with dead dealers whacked by the Nike gang in Finglas. A picture of his granny curled on a couch holding a bunch of chrysanthemums; monster Holy Mary in a Punto-blue dress peering down her seersucker top. Carol's shoe stuck in an antique trumpet. His passport. Loose turf. Sunglasses mounted on a Stanley knife. Pink edible necklace.

It was too late in the morning to leave the Old Bank. Pinstripe would be downstairs showing clients around giving it high-dough this and that. Sash windows, very versatile, safe room intact. De Valera lived around the corner. They locked horses on the towpath around the back, used to be a hotel, ladies with hats. Imagine what you could do with it now when the stock market gets back up, priceless mirrors. Legend says there's a ghost. Sixteen rooms up above; would make a great hostel, original Victorian chimney pots. Gonzo decided to hang on a while and have a wank.

He wanted to bang the nurse in the Mater who took bloods. He wanted to bang her cos she talked down to him. He wanted to bang her cos of the dirty way she leant over and smacked the vending machine. Big pillow tits blobbing all over the gaff and well she knew it and well the old codgers with the fucked hearts knew it and well the pleated receptionist with the tall latte knew it and well the trolley-pushing hunchback in plastic green knew it and well he knew it: they'd jelly wobble when he gave it to her goodo. She'd have to shut the fuck up saying shit about Hep-C, muscling, skin-popping, if Carol took mushrooms when breastfeeding the day the baby died. He wanted to bang her for saying things he didn't understand – subcutaneous – legs tied back with washing line rope so it could all slug out: Abrakebabra sauce on a big hot smelly kebab. He wanted to bang her.

He didn't mind what Carol did as long as no one came inside her. She'd be back with the scag in the afternoon, giving it the full candy, 'Darling baby I fucken love you, d'ye know dat? I'd fucken keel over fur yew.' They'd lie on the wet mattress after slamming the stuff. Then they'd green out and imagine all sorts. The two of them rolling into the hills biting sweat gashes off rivers, green slime, bits of broken helicopters, church bells in ears, cold tinny blue and God's feet, big as cheese urns, landing unceremoniously in a crumpled scared heap. The room would turn into a spinning fucken barrel turning shrill pork belly with them naked rolling and banging into the ridges with running whiskey gag. Wood burner he nicked farting out the leftover specks of fire on cling-film skin. When they'd come down with a crash twenty minutes later, she'd hear the ghost of the bank inside the old windows, telling her to pick up the horse shit and bring it to the man in the Botanic Gardens for the flowerbeds.

'D'ye hear him?' she'd say.

'Wot?'

'He's in here, talking again.'

'Course he is, shurrrup and he'll go away, fuck's sake!'

She'd hear the dead baby too, asking for his doo doo, 'Gimme boy doo doo, doo doo mine!' He'd have to pretend to hand the absent baby something, anything that might look like a doo doo. Then he'd slap it into her to get her to stop seeing the baby and she'd ask for another baby, tits well gone since they'd started using again. Looked like teacher's eyes squinting at the crap way he pronounced Irish words. Sometimes he'd bash them, but she never ever gave out about that.

'Gimme a baybeee, I want me babee back.'

He stopped bursting into her cos all three kids were reefed away by the social workers. No way would he be fucken doing that again, so he'd pull out and squirt on the wood floor. She'd slip on it going to the jacks and call him a wanker. Then maybe they'd fall asleep until the headerballs came by later, never knowing how to get up and in. He'd collect them on the fire escape, one by one. Lucky to have this place. Most had to sleep in the bandstand on the canal or in the laneway behind Doyle's that burnt down, sausaged in giveaway blankets with Leather Joe screaming inside night terrors of his ginger arse rape Da until the sun flew up over the broken roof tiles and car beeps gnashed at them. Pong of Spar hash browns, burnt dry and useless as donkey pelt.

By 3 p.m. the pains were ripping and no fucken sign of her with the gear, down the fire escape and out onto the North Circular hustling past the shops of shite. Quick glance down Goldsmith Street and onto more slice of side road. Every step up step down hurt like fuck. Fatsos by the cattle-cart stomping into Curves gym to the lyrics of 'I Will Survive'. He sang along to stop the pain from slit-sucking out his intestines. *And now you're back from out der space … I just walked in to find ye 'ere with dat sad look on yer face.* 'Come on now ladies, knees up and up and up again. That's it, keep going, let me see those legs moving!' Brenner in De Joy on the left, IRA prick, dying for Mother Ireland in a 15x20 exercise yard. The Mater Hospital with its wheelchair morgue; militia of swollen ankles. Around by the battered yellow flower shop and on and on. Holding on to his guts like a stolen Christmas present. Sweats horsing down under denim, face the colour of fresh snot. Passed the launderette where his Ma used to wash the boys' sports gear on a Saturday. 'Don't sit on the machines Patrick, what did I tell you Patrick, are you listening to me Patrick?' When he was just small enough to be growing that nose that would give him 'Gonzo' for all his days after. He'd probably never see her again. She certainly didn't want to see him again. Most days he'd clear forget what she looked like. He turned the corner onto Berkley Road and puked: a stream of moss-green gooey liquor, pouring onto slick brick, damming at a To Let sign.

'Look at de fucken state of him!' he heard someone shout out from deep underground. Then more voices. More laughter. More bawl. Someone shouting from inside the elderly sewers under Dublin filled with fibre optic cables, acorn turds, dead Vikings.

'Down here ye cunt!'

In the basement of the Spare Parts Shop the ugly bake of Dessie Kearney peeking up from his flat.

'Have you got any?' Gonzo asked. 'I'm in de bads.'

Dessie beckoned him down the spiral staircase. In the sitting room on the table, he could see the spoon. Skinhead in a Sideline jacket handed him a leprechaun cup of Nescafé.

'We can sort you out if you do us a fave,' Dessie said.

The drug scene in Dublin had got boiled-egg bad. Four friends in as many months dropped dead from bad score. Pyramids of empty syringes, citric wraps and codeine bottles stuffed into shores and mashed in doorways. Blister packs of Lyrica, benzodiazepines, ice, legs full of maggots. What couldn't be crushed down and turned into liquid was snorted, licked, smoked. From Talbot Street to Gardiner Street and down into the flank of docks to Fairview, casting into surf and howling out of rust-caked eyes into waves, sand shifting beneath drug boats, narrow little sea gods sucking at gravel and dancing a slithery leap. Low-cost booze and spat-back-up methadone from lippy whores was all you could see in the city centre before one o'clock in the day. Cops didn't give a gypsies as long as people like him hurried the fuck up and died.

He looked at Dessie who was eyeing up two lezzers on the couch. One of them, skinny as rashers, was pretending to grate her tongue. 'Yewer fucken gas,' her bird said, bending over for a sludgy on the cake hole. Both wearing dolphin necklaces, glitter leggings, squeegees of burnt yellow hair in bobbles of teapot spouts. He noticed they had front teeth missing as well.

'We need a drop-off of our gear up the flats at Baker's Yard. Cops are all over it. They won't know your ugly mug. Not many left we trust, int dat right Skinner?'

'I'm not doing the numpty for no fucken cunt,' Gonzo told them. 'Carol would brain me if I end up back in the slammer. She's not doing great after Charlie got taken from us and the other one not long dead.'

'Heard about dat,' Dessie said. 'This city doesn't have no respect for no one and yez were only doing yer bento to keep it together for those fucken kids.'

The day they came for Charlie was the worst stab in his heart ever. He saw Carol at the window of the flat from down on the broken concrete below. Foggy shadow of the social worker in navy behind her spilling the jib. Carol cocking her eyes towards the mountains, roaring and snotting, calling them all the bastards. Face pink as AstroTurf runners, nothing left but 'goodbye' to the little boy who slept in a cardboard box with two kittens that first winter they all tried to keep warm.

'There's pissloads of young bolloxes farting about picking iPhones like apples off O'Connell Street,' Skinner said. 'Muggings akimbo, robbed cars for €500, fucken break-ins. Dessie's been done here in the flat 'n all. It's gone mental cos of the cheap cut shite they're putting about. Guards clamping down like steel clips on a dirt-bird's nipples. But our stuff is good cack, it's the barley. If we get in with the Russians we'll have a chance making proper squids.'

Dessie butted in, 'If it goes A-OK Gonzo, we'll see ye alright when we get our glasses, know what I'm saying, do ye? We'd give you and Carol a bit of work if yezer game ball.'

Gonzo was afraid of Dessie even back in school when he lobbed custard out the window at muppets passing by. Chasing after seagulls on the Buckfast zig-zag, giving his fifteen-year-old girlfriend a black eye for buying the wrong smokes. Skinner was worse, he could tell. Grade-A psycho who'd snap your fingers off quicker than a fat kid at the zoo smashes a Kit Kat. Now they were turkey-chesting with Russians dealers, taking on the entire muscle-for-hire empire. Gangsters in silver puff jackets trafficking teenagers by day, selling pierced tits of an evening.

'Sandra here used to go out with one of the Russians, they're mad bastards, don't mess around. Tell them what they did to Stano …'

'This guy Andrei, right, a mate of a bloke I was with for a while, he nailed a fella's nuts to the floor cos he was four days late paying them.' They looked at one another as if to say 'that's enough'. Sandra started texting and snapped a pic of Gonzo's mug. 'They left him there, bleeding out for nine hours. It was rotten so it was.'

'What happened the poor fucker?' Gonzo asked.

'Dead as a dodo, what do you bleeding think happened him? He had two young kids and a new wife 'n all. It was in the *Sunday World*. They pinned it on the Poles in Ballyfermot but it weren't them.'

'Will ye stop with the fucking scare stories,' Dessie said, giving yer one the scaldies.

Today they'd sort Gonzo out. And he'd sort them out for tomorrow by doing a lemon flavour. Quid pro quo. No one need know. Take the stuff on offer first. Relax. None of them could do it. He was one of the few not doing a miserable scoop for a debt. Bob's your uncle. Fannywollop's your aunt. Twenty minutes later, bonbon church bells, ingots veins, stretched out on a divan with Skinner's spades spreading his furry cheeks apart to shove the drugs in.

'You've got a few hours so keep your nose down, get some grub, don't go into no pubs. If it goes roadrunner up yer hole after walking down, you'll need to go in somewhere and have yourself a shite. Just don't fucken wash the bags afterwards, wipe with a lump of jacks roll.'

He couldn't feel it much except for the arctic Vaso. They sat back on the couch and did the business, flopping like wankers for an hour or more. Skinner was right, this was good fucken stuff. Gonzo's brain felt like mushy peas in a polystyrene chipper box. He saw his Da playing golf with Jesus and that old bagalot from up the road at the green, Mrs Montgomery, riding an ostrich across the Hill of Tara with an old transistor radio tied to its neck. When he nudged back to life, the two lezzers were dry-riding against the back of the couch.

'Gwan,' Dessie said. 'Gerrup before ye crash, and watch yer fucken back out there.'

The city tipped down in a duck beak towards the Garden of Remembrance. Rain scattering Swarovski beads on the path as he plonked along. He thought of Carol's fresh face at eighteen. Cement angels leaned chin forward from Georgian chimneys. 'I'm out of me nugget!' he roared. Pains fostered out elsewhere now, he felt boundless, happy. Met her here with a gang of inner-city boys from the flats around Dominic Street, drinking cans and dancing to U2 songs on a ghetto-blaster sometime in the middle of 1994. She'd weight on her then, chubby sweet smile, horse-tail of hair whooshing from end to end in the sunbeams. They kissed for an hour without stopping: wet balmy tongue slosh he'd never done with any other bird. Sometimes he still felt guilty, but Leather Joe said, 'There's no stopping some, and ye never forced her to take it.' The counsellor from Rightways also explained that 'damaged people have a knack of stumbling onto one another no matter what.' It made sense that first time they tried to get off it together. Both their Da's were alcos and bashed them. Both their Ma's couldn't see anything wrong with their Da's, and bashed them. A few weeks later, they fumbled and gorged and slopped into one another under the flat-leaf bushes in the Gardens. 'What ye doing to me boy, what ye bleeding doing to me!?' Lads circling the railings, clutching chimpanzees, uuumphing them on. 'Slapper!' Afterwards, they took the piss saying Gonzo was a right grunter, like those fucken mating seals on RTÉ. 'It's you and me babe, no one else babe, you'll do me babe.'

At the edge of O'Connell Street where pigeons shat on the bloated head of Charles Stewart Parnell there was a big pile of cunts warbling the breeze about water charges. Slapper holding a salad cutter was screaming blue beam about not being able to pay her bills. A group of young girls, no more than five or six, carrying banners: WATER FIRST, AIR NEXT. Normally he'd stick around for the dip, but he'd only an hour and a half to get to the apartment and drop off the gear. Dessie warned him not to 'fuckarse about'. To get it done and dusted pronto. Skinner held on to his social welfare card until he got back. They doshed him taxi fare but he shoved it straight into his pocket for later. He was heading to the Wise Wok on North Earl Street instead. For a fiver you could nab a chicken curry that blowed the banana off. Thai bird with ladybird lips always lobs loads of vegetables in. He sat at the window gawking at the courgettes wondering how yer one shaved the sea-green bits off the edges in fancy crinkles. Wondering too why his boot of a Ma never bought broccoli or other mad shit when he lived at home. Stomach rumbling something poxy; he could feel the bunk beds of turds crumpling down. 'Fuck,' he thought, imagining turning up to the Russians with a whole load of shit covered in a whole load of shit.

He mozied out the door turning right onto Talbot Street. Reams of shouting shoppers nabbing cut-price bootle in Guineys. Roma pleb with a trumpet full of coins. Two alcos blocking the doorway at Dunnes Stores. It'd only take ten minutes to horse down to Baker's Yard. If he was in a bad way he'd leg it to the underground car park, reef the skank out his hole, finish with a dump at the side of some tosspot's Beamer before facing off the boys. Left right left right through the crowd shouting, 'Move will ye! Getouttameway.' When he reached the junction of Gardener Street, he was grabbed from behind, both arms, gutter knocked.

'Fuck's sake, stop it, I ain't done nothing,' he roared, But these were no cops and he knew on the fly they were wise to the stash on him.

'Shut it or you'll get it in the head,' one of them said. He had a foreign accent, smelling of pickles and beer. Another stood over him with the wrinkle tracks of his docs in full view ready to smack a print on his face. How the fuck could they know he'd be making his way down at this time? He thought of the two lezzers. Dessie had said he didn't know them that well.

Aulone in brown bandaged legs to the right shouted, 'Bowsies, fecking bowsies!'

He turned his head and twigged he was outside the pool hall with the painted bugs all over its walls. Whichever one peppered a punch and then a fuck of clatters he'll never know but his brain went bubbly. His mouth gassy and a thin veil of darkness shifted down from the next world to tell him he was a fly in the butchers about to be stamped out. Flipping menu boards rocked and crowed, scaffold poles on an old grey CitiHostel turned sideways to do a fiddler's jig. Punters slithered by not giving a fuck. He could feel his legs being wrenched along the damp cobbles. Shovel hands gripping his hoodie to keep his head from meringue cracking. He came to in a piss laneway propped up against a blue skip under the rotting planks of a railway bridge.

'You shit munching faggot fuck,' steel knuckles said. 'Who put you here?'

'I know fuck all,' Gonzo told them. 'I'm going back home to me bird is all, I know fuck all, fuck all.' He thought of the guy's nuts nailed to the floor, crying blood, no one lifting a finger to help.

Steelknuckle's mate, bloated as a Cosmonaut, took another punch, swatting him back onto a moss-slush wall. He reefed open his jacket and pulled out what looked like a shoehorn.

'You know what this is Oirish?' he said, rubbing the white bent-fish shape up and down under his nose. 'This is going inside your stink tunnel and it's going to hurt like your mama did when she pushed you out her blood sack.'

They reefed his arms and snapped them so fast Gonzo bent himself in half on a silent command. He was there backwards on the ground with Cosmonaut reefing his jeans down to the back of his kneecaps. He felt it scoopslide right in and up on over and back through sideways out again on up and down up in left slip up and on the turn back for a second go he hoped they'd whack him in the skull. His dead granny hovered like a helium balloon showing him her chrysanthemums, her apple trees and the pink flamingos her friend Betty brought back for her from Florida. 'Off ye go up there, have yourself a good look at the seagulls love,' she told him. 'Me fucken arse gran, me fucken arse!' He could hear them mumbling about the stash having gone up into him even further.

'Don't!' he roared. 'Fuck's sake, don't!'

'You don't shut up we cut your face off and make it into a mask.'

'We could feed this fucker to the dog, you like bulldogs Oirish?'

Cosmonaut pulled hard on the shoehorn getting the other knack to shove his whole hand in. Then quick as weather in February, they were gone. Already it would be a problem remembering what they looked like. Blood dripping from his arse, jeans ripped and just one shoe left upright against the skip like a bag of spuds.

There was no way he could explain this to Dessie, unless they fucken set him up rightly, but even that made no sense. He could already see Carol's head mashed open. These cunts didn't mess about, arms broken up like a discarded doll in the playground up at the flats.

'I'm fucked, I'm fucked!'

Two teenage girls pointing, laughing.

'Yez've no idea, I'm fucked!'

Up Henry Street with its orgy of phone shops and factory leggings and onto wet brush Moore Street. Last of the stallholders manically plying for trade outside the Euroscoff supermarkets that had colonised the gaff. On by Ballsy Bingo where his Ma used to take him long ago. All those mad bitches with Rothmans-stained chins shouting, 'Two fat ladies, go on Jimmy, get up and run, thirty one … dirty Gertie, clicketyclick, staying alive, eighty-five!' Some were able to handle four and five cards at a time, marking the numbers like Phil Collins on drums. *Bash bash bash.* He used to lie on his spindlies gazing up their skirts. Musty whiff of brown tights on an afternoon in November 1970-something. Disco lights, apples sours, Dusty Bin. Around by the broken Luas tracks up Parnell Street down to railings stuck with cat fur. Crossing barrister-brain Church Street towards home. No way would he be taking the usual route. Did he tell them where the squat was? Was he boasting about it before they iglooed his arse?

Carol would still be down at the Old Mill on the canal sucking off Leather Joe for a bag. Willy would be there too with the scab-ho wrestling over a lukewarm tin of Stonehouse, sucking her face off. Beamer the old tramp with the no veins. Hasslebat, his ginger eyebrows lighting up as hot worms in a snowy forehead. Smell of piss hacking the sun-up. Widearse Wendy with her tales of Berlin, before Guzz floated down the river with a bag of leaves in his mouth. Guzz who survived winters in Leeds in the 1980s sleeping under truck stop lorries, draining antifreeze through slices of white bread under the engine holes. Fuckface the Jack Russell in a rusty pram licking stolen satsumas. They'd be swaying by now, talking bollox, tapping passers-by. 'Scuzzz me scuzzz me scuwizzzzmeee. Do you want me to be like you? Is that it, do you want me to be like fucken you?'

'You're nothing but poxy trouble,' she'd say when he'd tell her what happened. 'Useless prick like ye. And ye gave them your card?'

His arsehole was stinging so much, he knew how she must've felt the first time he gave it to her up the jacksie. He'd to use HB ice cream to cool her down afterwards. Nothing would be the same after this. These were serious heads. Mavericks. Think nothing of using shooters. He was so stressed by the time he got to Broadstone he thought he saw a man snoring on a plank up a tree. Loped on towards Phibsborough. Maybe they'd be OK just hiding out in the bank. The rest of Ireland seemed to be doing the same. Stay gizmo'd there till he heard of them popped. All of them ones ended up popped. Time and time again, saw it rolling. He wasn't going back inside either, leaving her to her own devices. They'd have to lie there, not go out, till a different kind of light shined. Come out of charity, come dance with me in Ireland, that cunt Yeats said in the book by their mattress. But he didn't know fuck all about the skank or fiddlers like Carol, all thumbs and kettledrums, sucking off ghosts at the window in the Old Bank on Doyle's Corner.

Imp of the Perverse

We'd been in a doorway in a bad part of town after some module or other finished up and I said to him open up your coat there and let me give you a hug. It's Christmas let me in, I'd really like to give you a hug. And now that we're here, thanks so much for all your help. I mean it, no one knows their shit quite like you. Oh and I bought you some socks with Edgar Allan Poe's face all over them. They made me laugh, kind of funny but disturbing. Hope you don't mind me saying that, do you, you're not going to take offence? He had a reputation for being really savage if disrespected. He had a reputation for brute violence as well as epic romance. He had a reputation, this fucker. He'd got us to read 'The Imp of the Perverse' as part of the American Literature module, all about primitive urges. Impulse increases to

a wish, the wish to a desire, the desire to an uncontrol-
lable longing, and the longing (to the deep regret and
mortification of the speaker, and in defiance of all consequences) is indulged. Now I knew he couldn't stand me
but I also knew he knew I wanted something else from
him and everything had that awkwardness, that butter-
milk sky feel to it. I couldn't even look into his eyes for
long. There was just a lot of pressure there. I knew damn
well he wouldn't piss on the likes of me. It was all high-
end looks with an asshole like that. Pier glass women
reflecting back his lack of lacking if they were beautiful
enough. Oh God yeah, nursemaiding him at academic
conferences, pop star syndrome or whatever the fuck.
He had a load on the go. Well he'd the choice to have a
load on the go being who he was. Everyone talked about
it. How many does yer man need? Jesus, they must bump
pubic bones with the turnstile comings and goings. A
man like that must have to move house often. How does
he get a proper rest? Fair play to him though, fair balls
to him.

We weren't too long in that doorway when he said
we should move to another, around the corner away
from the bar where all the other students were drinking.
A minute's privacy *idée fixe* and I got a bit giddy and
said OKAY so OKAY let's do that let's go. In the other
doorway he said you really are very annoying but heaps
hilarious so don't lose that, humour's bloody important
in this game. He opened up his coat and in I went. Arms
right around his pure wool jumper nice and roasty with
the wind swirling and swooshing. Him clasping me back
nice and tight. The two of us, our broken breath, you

could hear it in the doorway there. It was so quiet I could feel the brick watching us. Passing beams of buses poking yellow fingers into our hair. His hands moved up a bit behind my back. Not so much rubbing but patting which I thought was a gas metaphor but then his nose went down a bit and mine went up a bit and I kissed him on the neck. I may have actually licked him on the neck to be honest I was so nervous. His skin warm and lovely like a chicken's out of the oven. I said you smell nice and he sort of smiled as his nose went down again and well I think he moved his hand up under my chin to raise me to him and then that was it. After all this time, this imagining, this critical kiss. Not sloppy which I'd expected: stupidly tender actually and really toasty, mad stuff, slow and soft too. Oh Christ can I say it? There was love in it, yes, a small snip of love that no one would ever get to find out about. He kept at it there with me, he didn't let up. Small persistent pecks then his lips rolling and lolling without moving off mine, very concentrated, yeah. His lovely butterball tongue pushing into my mouth as he kept circling my lips. Hands moving at a different pace in under our coats. Holding me to him. Fuck, it was good, like totally good. I began to crimple a bit, buckle. I wanted to say you're making me faint Chloroform Tongue. Oh Mister Chloroform. Instead I said finger me right now it'll be so eighties retro. I was trying to lighten the load. Rid some of the fizzy tension between us. When the air hit my crotch I realised how cold it was out there in the steel breeze of December, how clammy I was down there in satin knickers bought in May. Squirmed the worm and the toad we did. When the muffled moans came he sniggered like he'd achieved something. He had me. This man who'd go on to tell people how much he detested me. Yacking in dusty pub corners about how mad I was. Glaring across rooms and up stairwells. Or trying hard not to look at me. The man I'd tell everyone, including university staff, was a cold heartless wanker. The letter from him saying please leave me alone please. In that doorway we were happy. It didn't make sense. The fucker.

I took a few days off the course. Things were starting to shift. I emailed him: 'I think I may stay home tomorrow and just read. I suddenly feel like an immense sociopath, like I've scared myself or am jittery, a weird strand of massiveness.' He wrote back and said, 'I appreciate your engagement and honesty very much. Forget about the world today and treat yourself.' He sent a round-robin later on telling us to bring in a favourite lump of prose. 'Be prepared to present it to the group, just a few minutes outlining why the piece matters to you and how the author went about it.' Then I regretted not going in, all of them having him like that, me stranded at home wondering what it felt like. So much ugly craving. 'You've a real problem dealing with desire, you're priceless!' my flatmate Liz said. She worked in admin at the university but had the day off too. I told her straight up: 'He's burrowed in deep, you know? Occupying my mind. Limiting the scope of my thoughts. He's hunting me down on the landscape.' He could be one of those secret shamans. Hairy chest hanging out of a sweat lodge in the Wicklow Mountains, regurgitating his inner wolf. A darker edge, something a bit sickening. He probably messes about with Ouija boards. Or a sadist, I thought of that angle too. I could smell the ignoble off him. Then I hit her with the truth. I decided I was going to have his child and it wouldn't be human. Some pox-fiend of a son, pushing his diabolical animal head into my bladder. 'You need a good ride,' she said. 'Or a weekend in Berlin to rid the stress.' She got on with making the chickpea and sweet potato curry. I felt bereft, emptied.

All Christmas I was really messed up about it. The fairy lights flickered fool, you're a fool, some of them winking in a blue streak, all hypersonic and sarcastic. Liz had gone to her mother's, so it was just me and a few stragglers around with nowhere to go. *It's a Wonderful Life* did its warped splay of smarm on the telly and I roared no it's fucking not, we stand on the brink of a precipice, we peer into the abyss, we grow sick and dizzy for fuck's sake. I made Rice Krispie buns out of melted-down selection boxes. I imagined him sucking up Proust through a bendy straw on Christmas Day to remind himself how burningly intellectual he was. Some floozy cooking leftover turkey stir-fry for him on a burnt-out wok. Him snorting coke off her tits oh jingle bells all the way, yeah, how far off society's rules he was. He'd say that to some of his conquests, imagine: real life doesn't apply to me I just teach it, the fucker. When I was still good-student-brave he told me I had talent. To make sure to sign up for his course in autumn. 'I can't imagine it without you now,' he emailed. I said yes, definitely, I'd like to try out that Sex, Culture and Modernity course alright, it fits with what I'm trying to do. Love supranormal lit-junk, you know, animalistic lust, Gothic appetites and stuff, it's pretty sexy. *It is cold and within me the pain of desire makes me colder than I am comfortable to be. I draw my furs about me, a wrap of beige and black, broad stripes of caramel and ebony, with a collar from which my head rises like the neckband of a tiger-lily.* You have to believe this material is brilliant, edgy, he said. How many chapters have you written now (pulls ears back and squints)? I can help you with it. I know people, influential people to work with if they decide they can go ahead and work with you. Keep this up and you'll be published in a few years. Fine so, I said, that'd be great, but I'd love if you kissed me again, that's what I really want. No, he said, concentrate on your writing, stick with the task.

'Sweetness,' he texted, towards mid-January before classes started up again. 'Sweetness it's not your fault, let's meet. I overreacted. Keep it work-related, better for everyone. I don't actually read all of your emails, only the occasional ones when I'm in the mood.' There was no point being hard on him. Instead the most important crisis of our life calls, trumpet-tongued, for immediate energy and action. On the way to the hotel I thought about all the wonderful chalk talk in the English Department throughout the year, you know, stimulus for going forward. There'd be no need to mull over recent grievances. Our bodies were more than capable of expressing the tiniest thrills up to the most walloping that'd knock Electra off her feet. *Mourning Becomes Electra* by Eugene O'Neill, go read it, he'd instructed. We'll discuss it at the beginning of Spring term. It's adapted from the Aeschylus play, *Oresteia*. But talking is a liability, drudging to a genius like him, already swamped in words for a living. Lust has carte blanche, words do not. Be on time, he'd say too. The fucker was a real stickler for time. By Christ he could fling a dirty look! Sitting in a turquoise jacquard chair off the main arts block, watching grooves of students climbing the warbled staircase to the bockety second hand of the café clock. Despite his seething arrogance, he still struck me as the type that'd lose the nelly in an existential tantrum and hang himself one day.

Have you thought about the moment it all changes? The moment he makes it clear you don't have a choice anymore … You're his until he's finished with you … A gesture, a word, a look … He stood with his back to me facing the black velvet curtains, rectangular gashes of sunshine breaking in to light up the room. I tiptoed in my Red or Dead high heels towards the mahogany dressing table. Pulled out the polished metal chair. Parked my bum right there. He turned around and with no warning let rip a humongous watery fart. Cocked his leg to piss sideways onto the armchair that housed a pile of tourist crap; hotel menus, spare dressing gowns. The whiff was similar to the bags of hash Liz sometimes managed to nab, you know, mucky and musty maybe from grasses and meat festering in his gut. It certainly reeked of forest and wildwoods, thickets, wealds, dead things. His face was terrifying but gruesomely beautiful, yeah the fucker. Such a pronounced snout of grey-black fur with even furrier cheeks, wide forehead, exquisite yellow eyes that were of course teeming with filth and treachery. Oh what hadn't he pulled apart with his twelve incisors, four canines, sixteen pre-molars and ten carnassials on the landscape of his lifetime; huge feasts of cows, goats, sheep and salmon. Using his skill as a master scent roller, the art of olfactory camouflage to capture as many as he could lecherously dream up. What a disturbed greedy sap. Dances and bows. What a dangerous bastard. Dances and bows. He'd been producing sex hormones since summer but now was the time for stepping up dominance and all out severity towards the meek. He needn't have worried. I was rightly up for it, you know, like this was totally bonkers stuff. I stupidly thought we'd meet briefly, a few G&Ts, rabbiting conversation about bestselling novels and other experimental literature on the way. Trademark fumbles maybe. A half-mast blowjob against a gloss-painted radiator. But here he was Alpine stretched to the puckered ceiling, tearing off his leather jacket, shirt, jeans. Chest, arms and legs sheathed in two coats of thick hair, nipples ruby and bulgy as Haribo jellies. I pulled my kit off pronto.

'So, it's come to this for you and me?' he said, smirking. I wanted to giggle too. The Casanova cliché of it. Castigating me when in my bruised mind I'd done nothing wrong.

'Yeah, it seems so,' I said, looking sideways. I would not look at him directly. I was, I suppose, afraid of him still. Looking me up and down, tail in a low sway.

'How you getting on with work?'

'Fine,' I said.

'Any headway on the dissertation?'

'Not yet, still thinking exactly how to approach it, you know?'

He took a deep breath and stared. Something he does when assuming control. Pinning with his eyes.

'You feeling a bit shy? You're uncharacteristically quiet.'

'Cautious,' I said. 'Or suspicious, I dunno.'

'Of?'

'Of you. The way you shift. It's confusing. You can be a bit of a player, it's deliberate, right?'

He seemed pleased I was so anxious. 'Games are not my thing,' he said. 'Though I admit I can be playful at times, but that's a different fish kettle, relax.' He moved to the bed, patting the duvet. 'Maybe you should come over here.' How terrible and terrific this was all going to be.

I'd been in a musty wine bar over the Christmas break and there was this plonker he tutored on the art of acquisitioning women the year before us. Apparently he tells young women he's a school teacher, not a university lecturer. Age gaps never tolerated in reverse. Comment on their colourful clothes, their nips, their legs, their eyes, the smalls of their backs, their brains. Women like believing they're smart. Say it doesn't happen often, this mind-altering intensity. You never give yourself permission to feel this deeply. Too afraid of the pain. There's little point keeping in touch after a few goes. Move on. They'll go berserk, firing off certifiable texts, you've to expect it. 'It's an artform,' he cautioned. 'Handling the erotic imagination.'

'Have you told anyone about coming here?' he asked.

'No. How could I after that dressing down you gave me?'

'Good,' he said. 'That's good.'

'I can't figure out what you're up to,' I said. I really hadn't a rats how to handle him.

'What's with the attitude? [chewing wasp's face] You know nothing about me outside of a teaching environment but you seem to make a lot of presumptions anyway. And I hear you've been gossiping goodo.'

'I haven't,' I said, gifting him my best little girl face, eyes lowered. I was panicky about how much I did know. Gross things he did to get by in American cities when dispossessed as a PhD student. Two gorgeous slappers he shacked up with in Rome. Oh so polyamorous. Oh so philanthro-eroticist! Men he'd beaten the fuck out of in house shares. I even knew the kind of women's shoes he detested. What he liked to chew for Saturday breakfast: mouth open, brown sauce, no manners. Objects shoved up him at drug-fuelled parties. His dodgy politics. How he found his brother totally boring. His favourite sleepy town in Languedoc-Roussillon. Books that had made him mentally ill. I wanted to tell him I knew him comprehensively. I was practically his fucking biographer.

'Who can profess to knowing anyone at all?' I said instead. 'Just that I get the impression sometimes you can be a tad cruel, a bit of a *mé féiner*.'

'Why are you here then?' he asked, snottily. 'It's all the same to me if you stay or go. Do you want to be here?'

'You know I do,' I said. 'I'm here because I need to be here. Maybe we have the unfinished business thing going on.'

'I'm actually very kind,' he said. Really, I had to stop myself here. I thought of the stunning woman he humped on the first night of our North American Women Writers module in the summer term last year. The night we discussed Harriet Jacob's *Incidents in the Life of a Slave Girl*. Making a move on another student when we went out on the tear when it was finally over. Muscling straight in there in front of the first choice one, now discarded. Very kind fare indeed. I watched him do it from the sidelines, and he watched me watching him, that's the type he is. *I'd like to get to know you better.* Sure he had it off to a tee, and why wouldn't he?

'I don't doubt that you're the kindest of gentlemen, that you do your very best for your students, that you somehow genuinely believe this,' I said, grinning.

'Are you mocking me?' he barked. 'Are you fucking mocking me?'

'Jesus, no, I wouldn't dare, seriously, calm down.'

I was utterly throbbing at this stage. He could tang it. Fuck, his mental eyes. His blue robin egg eyes. That smouldering madness. Disgusting ire. The soreness spilling all around him. This tick of darkness between us. His seagull-in-flight upper lip. His nasty fucking demeanour. How I adored it. This bad thing that was always destined to happen. His Satanic odious octopus nasty fucking psycho self. What a shithead. Fucking hit me I dare you. Fucking bastard. Hit me just the once. Sharp smack to the face but keep your eyes on mine. Watch yourself doing it. Watch me. Hit me. Hit me hard I can take it. One big slap and keep your eyes there, right there. I want to see you when you do it to me. What have I done to deserve this? To deserve you? Hit me, please, I want you to hit me. Afterwards you can hold me. I'll hold you. We'll be close and I'll be upset. Holding on to you. Warmth of you. I love this. I want you. Your hot face in my neck; my hot face in your neck. Now look at that! We are closer than we could ever hope to be. But this is not anything near love. This is searing satisfaction. Get the fuck out. Out of here. Out of me. Fucking creep.

'Get down on the floor, crawl around,' he said.

'I won't,' I told him. 'I'd feel like a total plum doing something like that.'

'Do it!' he roared. 'Or I might up and leave.'

'I won't, I can't. Why should I?'

'You will. You should. You want to.'

'You're a crass stereotype!'

'Is that so? You really think that? Think you're a match for me?'

He came at me then, snapping, like he was in a teeming rage for feeling anything at all. I bit him on the shoulder but he quickly showed me who was Boss, didn't he? Oh it's funny, the diabolical fury. We stood shoulder to shoulder on the frontier asking will this, what if, should we? For a while it went mouse quiet, it was as if the fucker wasn't there at all. Then small yips and whines, quite sweet, unexpected. There we go. Sat up facing each other, lightly biting our muzzles, touching noses, nuzzling, bumping bodies, but nothing you'd call hotel hectic. We nibbled at each other's coats, tossing and tilting our heads about the place. Stopped for a small break and shared a bottle of sparkling Ballygowan from the fridge.

'You're not bad at sucking cock,' he remarked. 'But your nose runs and your eyes water, which is a pity.'

There was no time to answer. He shoved me back on the bed, smacking and pulling. 'You're a bitch who wants to be a dirty bitch, only a fucking bitch knows it.'

He flung his legs over my neck. Tail whipping in each other's shit as wolves do, pushing one out in front of him. The mess on those beautiful cotton covers, the stench! I hope he paid in cash. He clattered me a little bit with his forepaws, forcing me to drop onto front quarters into a crouch position. I didn't mind at all. Then he mounted me hard from behind. Belting and pounding. Yes, the swelling up inside was brutal, but I could see it was the type of sensual pain that'd morph into a primrose path once you're used to it. The sheer agony when he twisted to get us end to end, tied like that for a good half hour. Only thing he bothered saying afterwards was in the lift on the way out, he whispered, 'Your lipstick has worn off sweetcheeks.' I can't lucidly recall those tiny last moments. My bones really creaked, my pussy was sore. I do remember, however, his dark dismal head disappearing up the road. The flip of his long back. Sting of tail-swish lashing stray strands of night air. I'd watched it disappear many times before, wondering where he was taking himself off to. Who he'd meet. Charming nuggets he'd sling at bewildered yokes who lacked the basic emotional training to figure him out.

Liz wouldn't leave the steam mop alone. Plug-in cleaning implements were a way for her to deal with the nattiness of the world. Her hand clasped the trigger chugging and puffing steam all over the kitchen floor out to the border edges where the more complex dirt hid. 'You have to stop that scutwork and listen up,' I said. 'I'm worried about where you're at,' she said, 'terrified in fact.' I told her not to be, that it was all good. 'I have it. I'm on top of it,' I said. Scratches down my back and thighs looked like that of a crazed dog jumping briar hills to rid fleas. 'I'm not supposed to tell you this, it's confidential university business, but he's made a second complaint about you,' she said. 'A formal one this time, I've seen the correspondence myself. You're getting an official warning. Any further contact and you're off the MA.' I was stunned. I assumed a level of friendship … he told me it was alright to 'sound off' but you can never truly get what pulls a grenade in a fucker like that. 'This can't be happening,' I told her. 'He's my George Barker. Have you read *By Grand Central Station I Sat Down and Wept*?' She wouldn't stop glaring. 'He means so much to me.' She fired off a line about an appointment with the college counsellor. 'What's the bets his boozy Da knocked the bollix out of him and his Ma was a Valium-soaked thicko who lost contact with Planet Self?' I was trying to sound amusing, but sadness had already started to bobble. 'You've got to get a grip,' she said. 'You're fucking obsessed. You do understand, don't you, this could actually go legal?' By slow degrees, sickness, and dizziness, and horror, merged in a cloud of unnameable feeling. 'You should've seen the way he flanked me Liz, those hefty paws pinning me down.' I was now the problem that won't go away. His complaints building in number as his mind handily snapped and temper took over. 'Does he have a new girlfriend, is that it? I think I've seen her. Long brown hair, no make-up, gentle, obedient, the usual. That's not the kind of wanton madness we have.' Liz went quiet as a nun. 'I can't hear any more of it,' she said. 'It's nuts.'

There was just one shipwrecked moment in bed where I felt I'd got it all so catastrophically wrong. Wrapped, facing each other, relaxing, content. I saw in his facial expression an ordinary man, insecure and damaged, frightened from fighting himself for so long. I wanted to kiss him on behalf of every woman on the planet. Extract the darkness with a surgical scalpel. All that wrath, indignation, sorrow, the grated imprudent threats, differences of opinion, pettiness, dreadful public spectacles of pain, body parts sold to sleazy punters on city streets. All that wandering along roaring. Sick fantasies of rape and murder, of animals and even children. Piling more and more hate on himself just to stay screaming. I'd replace it all with chopped clear thinking. I wanted to say sexual jealousy brought me to this point and I'm horribly sorry. I've absolutely no idea who you are and I never meant for it to get so out of hand. I just wanted to make the grade. To be like all the others. For you to see me, notice me, fuck me, kiss me, want me, laugh with me, lie with me, cook me an omelette. This flick of jeopardy between us really is dangerous. We both know it. Let's not go there. Let's never go there. Let's look out for each other from a distance. A love story that never permits itself to fly off the ground or smack its face off the stars.

I'd rarely known such torment over someone I barely knew and would never know and I wondered what that was really about. The streets seemed to completely hack themselves of colour. Counteracting this was a new-fangled sense of smell. From Lower Drumcondra where we lived I inhaled the blood-spattered hospital waste in Holles Street 3.3 kilometres away. Sitting in Fagan's I was able to sniff severed fish heads down the docks and relish the tangy rust on the underside of abandoned cargo boats fastened to the Liffey walls. Light jilted and bluffed showing shapes of lonelier paths, judgements and views. With our son Bill growing inside me, I was learning how to shift posture, growl, glance. I did it with harmony and discipline, stood my ground and defended boundaries. I decided to build a den out the back about twenty to twenty-eight inches wide and fifteen to twenty inches high. I knew it wouldn't be long before I'd be sucking the veins of chickens from vans at the back of supermarkets. Spitting bones at charity shop windows. I sprinted to Woodies to get some supplies: trellises, ball grasses and potting grit. It was important Bill and I were comfortable. It was only going to be a seventy-five day pregnancy and I'd have to eat his shit from the den to keep it clean. He'd arrive with eyes closed, deaf and totally helpless. I stopped walking and began to lope, trot, gallop, at such speeds that my eyes drank in the zipping line of traffic with its silhouette of seated ant-heads. A pain in my chest wouldn't shift which I put down to the slaploads of raw meat I devoured daily. Bill's muzzle began pressing into me, causing me to piss on the move in the thick of spaced-out shoppers around Grafton Street and surrounding alleyways. By week three I stopped going out around the city and just stuck to the back garden. Liz's modus operandi was to totally ignore me, confident I'd tire of my camping adventure and take to being hominine once again, longing for the comfort of my king size memory foam bed.

She thought it'd be a good idea to have friends around on a weeknight rather than a weekend when everyone seemed to be terminally busy. The back of the house spilled down with LED light chains and solar-powered lanterns. Beef bourguignon bubbled away in a red Creuset on the stove rendering me delirious. I'd spent the week finishing off stocks of smoked salmon that had the perfect shelf life for outdoors but nonetheless gave me ferocious heartburn, forcing me to chomp the long grass. There was a shortage of large ungulates or hooved animals around the place, and of course muskoxen or exotic caribou. Cowardice had sidelined me to the neighbour's bins. I'd also started to smell really putrid. I watched the guests arrive, one by one, two by two, handing over tacky bottles of expensive wine, rabbiting on about their reasoned choices. They were exactly the kind of University People my love used to describe in his early emails: 'Lazy-headed snobs who love to sit in workshops only to improve their dinner party repartee.' Liz, the back-stabbing stool pigeon, pointing me out as the aberration in the garden. Gawping out at me, necks craned, forks suspended. I waved back to show that I didn't and couldn't care. Up until this I'd managed well. He hadn't tyrannised my head, not since his final crawling correspondence: 'I have no problem at all with you in the class. Quitting the course is entirely your decision.' I wouldn't let a mean-hearted fool like that mildew my mind or bonk my bones when it suited. He was the type to drop the trousers at any time of day or night. I don't know why he didn't think of sewing in a trapdoor to make it easier on himself. 'Desire is a public phenomenon, we've no right to resist it.' Fuck off you disingenuous bastard! Rather than lower himself to empathy or any notion of altruism, he'd sent even more missives. It struck me that he might not stop until he heard of me stone dead. One harped on about a photograph of my tits I sent him. 'Men do it all the time, we've grown to expect it,' I informed Liz, in a Post-it on the fridge. I dumped my laptop and phone so I wouldn't have to respond to further demands to meet with the dean. 'Cheek of that philistine citing my behaviour as *inappropriate* when he uses the course as fanny fodder all the time and no one blinks an ethical eyelid! You need to carry out a full internal review of your operations in there.'

I crawled back into the den and told Bill to treat girls and women with the respect they deserve by the time he reached a certain age. 'You're a hoot Mum,' he muttered back from deep in the willows inside me, 'but I've no idea what that means.' I'll teach him how to hunt but he'll have to pull his weight: hoovering, wiping down counters, chucking rubbish from the garage. There's no way I'm wasting my days lounging around playing with Lego, I'm not cut out for it. We'd start with smaller prey, work our way up to tougher flesh, rip it raw, eat it quick. 'When we're proficient enough, we're going all out after him.' Go for his cheeks where the tender flesh lives. Eat his grin too. His leather laptop bag. His sense of self. His monstrous ego. Eat his toenails. His house. His job. Eat the bus he travels on. Eat his whores, all of them, yes, every last one. His printouts. Eat his dauntlessness. The toilet he shits in. Eat the rashers from his fridge. Eat his funding opportunities. His comfy pub chair. His many works in progress. Eat his tactics. His belligerence. Eat his swagger. Eat his vision of the future. Eat his contempt for anyone who disagrees with him. His scornfulness. His fanaticism. Eat his entrails. Feel your father's icy chill creep through your pulpy heart and be glad of it.

I could hear the dining room door slide on its squeaky track and the legion of legs strutting out to the furniture. The gas lamps were hissing away matched in tempo by the gushes of the Cosmopolitan fountain we'd bought in a second-hand shop for a tenner. We'd got it originally to celebrate my last day at the university. On that day I'd only downed half a glass when I got the urge to sneak up the stairs and scrawl *KARMA* on the whiteboard in his lecture room. Liz was there in a flash, my praetorian guard, eraser in hand, the usual efficiency. 'Leave it please,' I said. 'I need this one last clump of counter-play.' All those pregnant sentences in his Inbox that consigned me to the hangman and to hell. 'It's over,' she said. 'Is it fuck!' I replied. 'Even if it takes five years, I'll be back for his balls. That man always underestimated me.'

In the garden I watch the guests through the heat of amber eyes. Grasses bristle and jostle. I stretch forward to lie flat in the flimsy sunshine of early evening. The clouds are hungry and my mouth waters. Wind tears at itself as

I pull layers from the sky to lay over me. Laughter grey and mocking. They do not know the danger love carries. Inside my son scratches and grows. I retract his moans back from the patio glass in a tender flow of light, creating a partial vacuum to insulate against emotional prowlers. They do not dare and should not dare, not here, not near. I'll rip them up. Licking and guzzling sick sour flesh. Springy muscle lathered in so much cloth. Juice of small succulent eyes. I'd gladly slash him in the same savage way. Licking, guzzling, digesting. Scorched screams in the small hairs of hell's ears. Viscera of him, black and full of distemper. Vital organs crawling with lies. What would he say and how could I begin to understand it? Trees move, insects move, birds move, nothing matters. Sounds from out around the suburbs cannot distract from the pain. Horns, planes, cackles, barks. The screech of tyres on dry pelts of roadway. There is no let up to the wind. Loneliness stirs, shy and submissive, among the branches. Anger rises. It rises with such intensity I see its violent head, shaking. It flings me into the den. Forces me onto my back. Flash of fangs. I throw myself into the fray. What is this chorus of urgent plaintive howls? Aloneness deep and dark. I lick it, groom it. Snarl, scurry for cover. Tattling to keep it all under control. I could dig all night to go deeper, a shallower pit, only to find it's still not the right spot. Only to find new clumps of dirt blocking the entrance. I am hardened now. Disrespectful towards the length of human days. Finally sleep arrives. Cavernous sleep. Squatting down in the treacherous hollows of the mind.

SOMAT

I was a controversial case. Even before Beard met Opus
Dei met Speculum Man. Grey hospital cubicle punched
with derma-grip, iodoform fungi, yellow tiles. Peter
Papadoo giving it the: 'No more babies!' His job is not so
much a sure thing anymore. He worries she will not cope.
I hang above the flare; nail fur, metallic ale, unmoored.
Knapsack of neurons showing me where to plop out
on any given day. Mama goo goo-ing: 'We'll get by, we
always do, go with it, get on with it, it's all good, don't
freak the beak.' Sleep brining sleep, reflex arc, breathe,
swallow, lick. Magus of my future, she is packed with
a million woolly things to say to me. 'My butter fairy,
nincompoop, my pickyuppy squidgy monkey. You will
not stop running around. For the love of Jaysus. Oh you
with the cut knees! What are we going to do about you?

Rascal flower, pumpernickel. There's no stopping you! Why would I want to? So cuddly-do. Let me squeeze that sweet gooey centre of you. Come here to me now. Don't make me run! Would you look at the getup of ye.' Then it happened: I heard no more from her.

Peter Papadoo rushes in looking like a right ball of shite. Straight from work. Slathered in muck and leaves. 'This can't be fucking happening,' he says, apologising, all a-fluster. Looking for an in-the-know, big league doctor, an expert, an un-doer of crummy miracles. Awful sorry, so sorry, *sinfonietta* of sorry from a lot of mouths. 'A terrible thing though very rare, but I'm afraid it's now a definite'. Staff nurse crumbled in disinfectant grips him. Into a foggy cubbyhole. Flicks a chart that shows exactly how it can happen. A laminate chart. Team arrive. She won't even take Panadol for a headache. Ran two mini marathons last year. Not a bother with the other three. How can this be? 'It's rare, but not exceptional,' Dr Falvey tells him. 'We need to take her now, immediately. You wait outside. Someone will be with you as soon as we know more. We need to move now, sharp.' Plastic doors plash a sulk of dead air. This is what it's like when the planet putters out its last dingy light and a lone animal wiggles in the flourishing fade.

Beard rubs his nose with a peach linen hanky, eyes streaming. Wash away irritants, scratch, piece of grit. Paces the virgin PVC floor. Flicks pen top in out, out in, sterling silver. Hippocrates used silver to treat ulcers and wounds. He calls them over. Points to the machine. 'Bring me through it,' he says. 'Bring me through it.' 'We suspected it was related to epilepsy but …' No, not you

Dr Falvey. Her. Step up. 'Is this the appropriate time?' Dr Falvey asks. There's little time. Her family is outside. It's exactly the right time. What else are they here training for? Inches forward in rumple-toe shoes; Nurse Bernie from Skerries. Pure gas at karaoke and never wanted to be a nurse but for her broad-shouldered adoptive Ma who took her on by the grace of God and claimed it as a sound idea. 'The scan shows a blood clot.' I can see that already, Beard says. And what else? What about intracranial blood flow, other vitals? 'It's not good,' Dr Falvey butts in. Let her answer, I'm asking her. 'A massive stroke on top.' On top of what? 'On top of other internal injuries.' But are they classed as actual injuries? 'What do you mean?' It's not a trauma per se, so what is it exactly? 'Brainstem death,' Nurse Bernie says, her knees buckling. 'Excuse Bernie, doctor,' the other wispy nurse whispers. 'She's also pregnant, a few weeks in.' Well this is how you learn. Get the family in pronto. I also need to speak to Boyne ASAP. Girls, wait, girls, listen up, it's also classified as whole brain death, not just brainstem death. Make sure to know the difference. There's an important medical distinction here. Baby is still with us. Heartbeat strong. What's the husband's name? Go find Boyne. As hospital manager this is totally his ball.

Peter Papadoo shuffles in with Grandpa Brian. Brief relief that she is now in a room of her own behind reception, tucked away from the beeping ant stream. 'My sunshine, my beautiful lil' sunshine,' he says in a slurp voice, touching Mama. 'You who were always so stunning, no less dazzling now.' Peter Papadoo starts to sob. 'Don't Brian, don't.' When we took her home from the hospital she slept for a month. We thought there might be something wrong then. She barely drank a sup. Then overnight didn't she sprout up a big pink hibiscus. Tallest in her class at age six. Nicknamed the Spinning Pea because she could never sit still or do one thing at a time. She started up her own dance troupe of young 'uns, did she ever tell you that? The Beaumont Belles! Prancing around the dining room table in a heap of made-up steps and flounces. Leader of the local litter club, scrubbing up them filthy laneways at the back of the estate. Mother to I don't know how many gerbils. When she was fourteen she came back from a school trip to Paris having spent all her money on presents for us, every last blasted coin. That's the type she is. Thermometer of the Eiffel Tower on a Bakelite base.

She does not look good, not good, not good at all. Her bones splinter when her limbs are lifted. There's a piece of mould growing from her head that looks like a clouded wedding bouquet. Falvey brings in a consultant from outside. 'Numerous infections, the eyes won't close. She needs ongoing everything, there's talk of meningitis, drugs for the bowels, the stomach, a series of slow flows. She needs to be turned on the hour, it's …' Stop you there,' he says. 'I have never seen the likes. In all my years, across many countries. What have they said of the legislation exactly?' There's no machine on the planet that can keep this up. What is the confusion about? 'It's complex,' Falvey says, without being sure exactly. Sometimes that's how complex complexity is. He thinks of the vending machine Oath they all took with no sub-clause for the good poisons that might squall a swell as big as the Hill of Tara with dolmens and dirt tracks underneath. He thinks of his own daughter bouncing on a space hopper. He thinks of banshees and their pneumonic screams, how they are specifically designed to scare young boys. His mind turns to golf. There is so much tediousness and yet nothing more to do here. He takes his own blood pressure.

The media is assembling, queuing in their cars on the tar. Remember no cameras, just facts. We're not that sick. Have a good look at the Texas Futile Care Law, it's not so dissimilar to ours. No opinion pieces, leave that to the idiotic blogosphere. If there's only 20 percent chance of survival at twenty-four weeks, what hope has this mitten at eighteen? Is there anyone out there who's prepared to talk openly on this? A similar case up North maybe? Get a flaky feminist to do a lawnmower mouth on it. What are the doctors saying? Are we talking severe handicap or stillborn? How far is the State willing to go? Where is the precedent? Get an intern down to the courts, always murmurs in the corridors there. Follow the cloaks, no cacking off to Guards, keep it lean, a crisp 800 words.

Owen refuses to come to the bed. There is a wail inside his stomach that wants to plaster the walls of the world with hot pins. She is asleep too long and he can't sleep at night as a result. He never thought her to be so mean. Isaac broke so many of his toys in these two weeks, the longest running hours of his life. Even the wooden tractor bought in Galway beside the pie shop where daddy burnt his mouth on a slimy red pepper. Instead he watches the drift of skirring seagulls on Dublin's skyline, so far up the clouds look like soapy blobs that slip off the scrubbing brush in the sink after dinner. 'Why didn't Edel come with us?' Isaac asks Peter Papadoo, though he takes a little while to answer, explaining she has a snuffly nose and doesn't want to give Mama a bad cold. 'Is Mama trying to be inside Halloween?' he enquires. 'Her face looks like the pumpkin we put on the windowsill in the sitting room except for the colour.' Peter Papadoo clasps an arm around him into the tightest of hugs. The most crucial thing about being a boy of his age is to be brave at all times, to push on like a musketeer in a jumbo maze of briers. 'Can we get crisps from the machine?' Give it a minute or so more. Talk to your Mama there, tell her what you've been up to. 'What's the point?' Owen pipes up. 'It's not like she can actually hear us or maybe she doesn't even want to anymore.' No, no, no, no, no, that's not true! That can't be true and will never be true. She is just not well. It's not her fault. You do understand it's really not her fault? 'Yesterday Owen bashed the machine in the hall when the chocolate wouldn't fall out proper,' Isaac tells him. 'That's totally not true!' Owen says. 'You are making things up all the time Isaac.'

The simpering PR guy shows Peter Papadoo and Grandpa Brian how to use the Tassimo in time for the meeting. 'Pop a pod in there – Samiaza or Café Hag are pretty good – but of course it's up to you.' Grandpa Brian has his eyes hooked on the unperturbed frosted head of Boyne sitting at the long rectangular table at the very top of the room. 'I'm not in the mood for refreshments,' he says. It was all 'tragic and unfortunate … difficult, and challenging' until they put it in writing they wanted the life support switched off. Now they were being summoned to several 'briefings' per day. Talk of 'viability' and 'potential legal consequences'. Host of other fruitless buzzwords and lardy sentences stuck snug in a worn book. 'Look at the state of them,' Grandpa Brian says, pulling at Peter Papadoo's elbow. 'It's looking more and more like the Last Supper every day.'

Dr Falvey outlines what he considers to be equitable fact: mechanical support is normally only used to keep organs intact until such a time as donation is feasible. Absence of neurological activity, already determined, is legal death. In his opinion, if he may be so bold as to state it out loud right here, the Eighth Amendment shouldn't even come into it as she's already gone. Boyne cuts him off as he would a hunk of ribeye. 'It is not our job to stand on top of the law, but to serve beneath it.' Grandpa Brian reminds them that legal submissions will be heard in the morning, it will be more obvious what way to go. 'According to your own paperwork, she was very much looking forward to the birth of this child,' asserts Boyne. 'Of course she was!' Grandpa Brian replies. She had chosen names. She had decorated. She had made provisional enquiries at the same multidenominational school the others go to. The child's presence in the world was almost tactual, tangible, inasmuch as her roaming heartbeat was. 'We are heaps ahead of the United States,' Opus Dei says. 'They don't recognise such a right until it's out and about sitting on the ground looking and smelling like a baby before it's deemed to officially be one.' Grandpa Brian and Peter Papadoo don't care if Ireland is an ejecta blanket of ignorant moon and the rest of the world is an even rougher surface still, they cannot and will not change their minds. 'It's about dignity,' Grandpa Brian informs the table. 'Our resolution is as solid and still as she is.' Boyne shuffles his papers. 'We have to be very careful here not to confuse relative with absolute value on human life, while of course trying our very best to do right by your daughter.'

Floppy liver strapped to chrome and fibre plastic in a cleaning closet on the fifth floor. Sanctify me in a sick bag. The next incy step for ethical kind. Gashed from Mama at night five days ago, Speculum Man who delivers premature babies with distinction and expert of women's parts; Beard, with the aid of Boyne's blind eye, decided it was the only way to save me from fire. They plan to grow me for twenty weeks and see how it goes. In a few weeks I'll be plump enough for a tube through the nose into the windpipe, a mix of air, oxygen and prayer. Dr Falvey will be pulled in to see me this afternoon though they have the colour of him in advance. His Facebook page shows just how much of a rancid cause carrier he is: Royal Society for the Preservation of Marine Animals, Doctors for Gaza, Great Apes Survival Partnership, No Fracking Europe, but barely able to look management in the eye or answer his wife back. He'll keep his mouth shut alright. 'O, God! O, Jesus Christ! No! How is this possible? Pure monstrous!' Beard will explain a gorgeous filthy irony – new technology from an abortion clinic in Canada – where there's no restriction on gestational limits, an exodus in reverse. And don't start going down the calculable line of Frankenstein, for pity's sake, who else will give a flying shit about me!? The country is run aground (they are saying), abortion under certain circumstances will be all circumstances before too long.

This is our only chance to prove the body politic wrong. Think ahead to the golden moment, where we present our findings. The look on their faces.

A legal envoy from the courts is set to visit to clock my heartbeat for a flipchart, except I'm no longer where he thinks I should be. They will probably take a line in from another, between 120 and 180 beats per minute, steady whoosh of citizen. No visitors allowed in to see Mama now under any circumstances, because she is, let's be very clear about this, not in decent fettle. Stew meat that's been on too long, melting collagen, thawing into gelatine. Peter Papadoo can't bear to look at her face, the smile of his saucy brunette having flown the nest for sure. Her voice follows him about the house in every cupboard he opens. 'Will you just try to fold the clothes for once, not fling them!' He's down at the courts most days flagellating and flailing, trying to grab as many legal eagles and politicians as he can. 'Our hands are tied,' they tell him, with shoulder pat. 'But it shouldn't be too long now.' Grandpa Brian is burying underground, eating soil, hiding from the bloodthirsty mink as he sees it. Dr Falvey uses the phone in reception to join a tennis club. It has brand spanking new Tiger Turf that's resurfaced every year and you can play under floodlights seven nights a week. Mojitos cost only €6 for members.

She's come to get me. 'Rascal flower, butter fairy, there you are! Come here to me now. Don't make me run after you!' Unhooking tubes like you do with a baby seat in a good-sized family car. Messianic puddle on the floor is all that's left. Experiment over, hypothesis incomplete, breakthrough broken. 'You don't mind, do you, if we hang around for a small while?' Mama says. Daddy is in a right fluff and needs our support. 'Look at you! You are cuter than I thought I could ever do! Is that not a Cheshire Cat smile? Also I think it would be good for you to get to know Owen, Isaac and Edel a bit better. They're all so different … delightedly themselves. It sometimes pinches the breath right from me. Good God, they will go nutso for you though! Be prepared. Edel will likely put dresses on you. She really wanted a sister.'

Boyne's wife turns up at the hospital at the chink of dawn for a good aul bicker. His own fault for not picking an equal. He has not been home since I went missing. She thinks he's having an affair. To her it's a matter of plausible explanation. She discussed it at length with the other ladies at the gym. It's not that she's totally thick but certainly she wouldn't have even a quarter of the brainpower as him. He told a colleague when he met and married her it was all a bit of a package deal. Measure for measure, tit for tat, tooth for tooth. He'd done that 1980s' thing of spotting her across a packed dancefloor: 'That's the woman I'm going to marry!' She has zero concept of the pressure he's under now. Volumes of paperwork alone would depress an Olympic diver. Skill of skills to stop a post-mortem too. If it gets out he'll lose his bonus or even worse: there'd be a sticky public enquiry. He leaves her to the front door by A&E, kisses the sacred space between her cheek and chin and watches her disappear into a pack of parked cars. She understands now how exhausted he is. She may have made another dumb mistake thinking otherwise. The sun is back out from her skirt shadows. He pops that awkward small bone in his neck before strolling back through the double doors towards the waiting mob.

The Glens of Antrim

He gets in touch with the moniker 'Ivan Campbell' and says it's an old email account he only uses to send hate mail to local politicians. Says something along the lines of you were never just a hole to me and that email from Marcus back in the day was indefensible. Nobody has ever kissed me the way you did in that old house in Belfast … sorry I hurt you, we were all fucked up beyond recognition. I ping one back with the subject line 'Coolio Babycakes' explaining that I'm living with the other guy in Dublin now, and he'd have to ask permission! Finally I crack a joke about how natural it feels driving a scooter gripping both handlebars. Why do people spin the breeze holding only one? Oh you were so good at that, he types back, the very best. I can't help but smile. Back to the salt mines for us so, I tell him.

From: Ivan Campbell <666ni@yahoo.co.uk>
Sent: 06 June 2016 16:39
To: Rosie Dew
Subject: Re: Those salt mines

Yes, we're all dark and intense up here. A mixture of miserable winters and a terrible history. Like Russia only with Orangemen. Truth is my life is suburban and fine. I do DIY, work on cars and boats … really I should go and live in Arkansas. Kids are well and my twin daughters are now sixteen, excelling at school being regularly first, second or third in a year group of almost two hundred girls. I am justifiably proud of them. The wee man, now seven, is going to be an actor. He's naturally dramatic; loves reading and goes to drama class as well as judo. Maybe he'll be the next Bruce Lee or Steven Seagal. I have great sex with my wife from time to time. We found the key to it, but it's infrequent, which is a pity. I gave up swinging the same time as I gave up cigarettes, a true test of will. Still think of women a lot but haven't sucked anyone's cock since way before the last time I screwed you, however long ago that was. Although I remember it was straight after you'd got out of the bath, you came down and lay in front of the open fire in the living room. You were, unusually, stark naked and your skin was still damp and warm. That was incredibly sexy. Who was the 'mad bint' you talk of, what was her name? I'm sure her kids were okay for food. Those little loyalist tykes are on fish suppers straight off the breast.

An estate agent is what he was supposed to be when he swanned up in the slick navy Audi in his pinstripe suit. In turn I would play the bored solicitor's wife on the hunt for a country pile. 'Wear a tight Lycra top with your tits hanging out. Purple lipstick, black trousers, heels, a smart jacket. I want food or dirt in the cleavage. You're unintentionally slovenly and that'll be dealt with later when you're tied. There's a postcard of a naked woman on the dashboard. She's leaning on a chair, pointing into the distance. There's a pillbox hat on her head and a small snake wrapped around one ankle. Study her as we drive off but don't mention her. Don't look at me either until I pull up at a chosen location. Only speak when you're spoken to. If you laugh I'll put you out of the car. Are we clear?'

He'd called around for the first time three weeks before. Part of the deal was he'd bring a toolbox and whack up some picture hooks and a large red canopy above the bed I'd bought on eBay for a tenner. 'Well here we are,' he said when I answered the door. Tall, tanned, green eyes, wide lips, smelling of Palmolive soap. 'Shit, this is real,' I giggled. He seemed irritated. Pushed by me into the sitting room, swinging open the metal box, getting to work straight away. 'Where do you want them?' I sidled off to the kitchen to get a glass of prosecco. He wanted cold beer. The counters were rubbed clean with lemon wipes but out the window at the side passage the mounting bags of rubbish were starting to attract fruit flies. 'Do you take anti-depressants?' he asked. Pressed against the counter he nudged his tongue deep into my mouth. I felt dizzy quite quickly, if not a little sick. He stopped and told me to 'breathe' before going again. His hands kneading the back of my hair. 'Can we just … can you hold on …' He pulled back to look me in the eye. 'What's that smell?' There was a fish pie in the oven. 'I thought we might eat,' I said. 'I'm more of a bacon butty type.' There was no meat in the house. 'Take off your top.' I can't do that, I told him, I'm shy. 'You're in chatrooms looking to fuck strangers, but you're a coy little girl, am I getting that right?' He pressed me up onto the counter, rooting his hands down my knickers from behind. 'Can we just go to the bedroom,' I said. 'Really, it'd be more comfortable for me.' There were leftover eyelids of radish in the salad spinner I bought in Arnotts, winking at us. The downstairs toilet fan whirred in disapproval. It seemed to go on for a good bit and I got embarrassed at how wet I'd got. 'You go first, dirt before the brush,' I whispered, at the bottom of the stairs. 'Do you always feel the need to make crass jokes?' In bed he made me beg but I couldn't manage it without laughing. 'I won't stop with my hands until you invite me inside properly.' Rarely had I felt so crazed. 'Oh just fucking stick it in, please!' Afterwards he made me sit on the top step and stretch my greased fingers up towards the landing light so he could examine them. When he left I felt shaken and tired. The crust was so hard on the pie it was inedible and there was nothing else to eat until the Tesco shopping arrived the following morning.

From: Ivan Campbell <666ni@yahoo.co.uk>
Sent: 08 June 2016 11:22
To: Rosie Dew
Subject: Re: Re: Those salt mines

Salt mines, salt mines … Are you sure they were salt and not iron ore or uranium or something? There are abandoned iron ore mines in Glenariff and Glenravel (just two of the famous nine Glens of Antrim) and we went for a walk once in Glenariff through the trees so that seems likely. As for cliffs near Larne, I think you are imagining that precipitous knobbing scenario as well, confusing it with a story I told you about my wife perhaps? The only clifftop overlooking the ferry out of Larne would be the back of F. G. Wilson's generator factory, which I am sure has seen plenty of action in its day, but not, alas, by me. I did do you on a bench in a little wood once. Which was nice. I'd love to fuck you again, orgasms or not. Doubt I'll ever forget that night you almost came. It was freaky but also very powerful, whatever was going on with you. 'Please don't, it'll kill me.' Christ that was intense! You were also surprised when Katie came, saying she found that hard too. Then again she was off on some pimp-choke fantasy and I had my hands tight around her neck at your request. Takes all sorts. Oh and any time I'm introduced to a woman wearing Angel perfume, I get a massive erection, so thanks for that …

The scenery was hairy, lumpy, very beautiful. He drove like a motherfucker through it. The red of the fallen leaves looked like blood spatters from a mouldy green Cyclops above. Gushing water from high up in the armpit of the hills was audible even inside the car. His legs bobbed with the changing of the gears. What was I doing in Northern Ireland? Who was it for? Was it a man? Of course it had to be a man. How was I surviving financially? Was I kept? I had harlot-red lips after all. Was I also interested in women? It'd be good practice if I wanted to take this kind of thing seriously. The man was married, had I fallen for the whopper cliché? Low self-esteem. I wasn't

what he would consider conventionally good-looking
at all. Sexual magnetism, maybe, but understated. He'd
been looking for someone to fit the bill for a while. A
spoilt wagon. Ripe for a good hard spanking. Volatile
bitch. Maybe the other man I'd moved up for could only
meet once a week. Kinked up and waiting to make him
feel special for a few dusk-musk hours. How many stints
in psychotherapy exactly?

The nude woman with the snake on her leg looked
brothel-weary; cardboard tits bobbing to the contours of
the wood chip on the forest floor. She had an amazingly
flat belly (they all did then) and her snatch was concealed
from view. She probably had to work as a deckhand
servant in the mornings. They're the bits you don't see.
'When I pull over you're going to get out, walk around
to my side, open the door and suck me off.' I wasn't
going to do anything unless he kissed me. That's what he
was best at. 'Snog me first, otherwise it'll taste all wrong,
like under-grilled halloumi.' He wasn't best pleased. I
was now 'in training'. There would be assignments, house
chores, porn clips to analyse, costumes, fantasies to pen
down. There was equipment in the car including a sling
of some sort to yank my legs back. He knew about the
operations. But I wasn't to complain. Never complain.
The whole world was complaining all of the time. This
was about taking responsibility. He needed to be able
to see more. The only training I'd had was a secretarial
course in the late eighties that landed me a filing job in
a pet insurance company in London. There was also a
speculum, some shackles, cat o' nine tails, bubble wrap.
He'd shave me once a week: smooth as a flaked almond.

I'd give him a house key. We walked through the trees a bit more and he asked to take a photograph with my head turned towards the hills in the paling light. He glared like a badger. Took the postcard out and began to stroke himself vigorously. Before he came on the Victorian lady he strolled over and removed the popcorn from my cleavage that I'd placed there that morning before we set off. On the way back to the car he completed his estate agent brief by showing me a few sites to build a dormer on. The next day I woke to a stranger looming large at the end of the bed. 'This is Marcus,' he said. 'He'll be here to clean the cum off you occasionally.' He looked like an IT goon, a manager from IBM. Yellow hair, yellow teeth, long piano fingers. 'Put this cushion up under her arse and we'll take a good long look at the tawdry slut.'

From: Ivan Campbell <666ni@yahoo.co.uk>
Sent: 09 June 2016 08:15
To: Rosie Dew
Subject: Re: Re: Re: Those salt mines

Those signs are pinned all over Co. Antrim, less so in the other counties. The story is that it was a single Presbyterian minister on a bicycle who went around nailing them up over a period of fifty years or something and then after his death other evangelicals took over. There are definitely fewer than there used to be. Strangely, I saw one on Friday driving the back road from Ballyclare to Larne – 'Eternity Where?' – and a bible reference, which is a pretty common one. They sprang up again about ten years ago after a couple of hysterical newspaper articles about dogging in broad daylight. It caused a public outcry, especially at Gleno near Larne, which I could never see being a spot for that sort of thing. The tower (or something) could be any number of things. I took you to Tardree Forest on the off chance we might see some dogging action, but we didn't. Was very glad at the time because I really couldn't tell if you would have wanted to join in or not and I wasn't in the mood for that sort of craziness that day. For the record, I was never annoyed with your bloke. I never met him so why would I be? I always thought good luck to him, you're a handful!

My appetites began to shift. I wanted more and more penetrative sex, but without the gimmicks. The Masters online were nothing like him. They had long grey ponytails and rotating wheels in their garages with nipple-clamped pony-girls on permanent spin. There seemed to be a lot of pain involved that didn't appeal to either of us. Stretched holes that wouldn't look out of place featured on *The Sky at Night*. Women with stunning svelte bodies getting the shit knocked out of them. Candle wax, pins, ropes, the works. 'Turn it off, please,' he said. 'That's a whole other level of zany, utterly depressing.' The floor was strewn with leather and latex drudge we'd stopped using. I couldn't walk the circumference of the bed anymore without stepping on a spike or slipping on an anal douche or plastic paddle or gloves bought in the joke shop as part of a French maid outfit. 'I feel miserable,' I said. 'You just don't seem to give a fuck.' He was gathering his things, crab-plucking them into a stripy sports bag, looking everywhere but at me. 'You need to calm down,' he said. 'What would you know about women's needs?'

I replied, showing him the emails from the men who'd written back. He didn't seem keen for others to join in. He wanted me for himself, but he didn't want me at all. 'It'd be wholesome,' I insisted. 'Nourishing even, to have three or four. I've seen clips where the woman sits on a hotel room stool and just reaches out for the langers like she's learning to play a spectacular new instrument. It'd be intense.' I wondered if the women who got involved with hardcore types started off like this. Did they consider it domestic violence out the other end of the sausage machine? Did they even have a choice? 'Consensual kink, that's what they're calling it,' I said. 'Can you fucking believe it?' He didn't answer. 'There must be a sex school in a doorway up over a shop on the Malone Road somewhere for repressed women, to take them in hand, you know, to teach them how to cope.' He was becoming an anorak. 'Have you ever considered doing Pilates or aqua aerobics, something to just get out of the house?' Marcus had apparently pulled out. Grown scared of me. Worried about his wife finding out. Everyone had a wife. The men in the ads were trying to talk me out of it. 'Why would you do this? You seem like a nice girl. Get yourself a proper boyfriend. Take it easy.' It morphed into a feminist issue. Misogyny. No one was listening. The stock exchange had crashed.

It was a good while before I saw him again. By then I'd moved to the Manor house by the sea at Whitehead, taking on a poetry course at Queens. His face was more rubbery than I remembered, he was slimmer, not so tall. I pulled him by the jacket sleeve through the enormous entrance hall to the dual-aspect lounge which still impressed every time I strolled through the rickety door frame to the splat of polished oak floors. Got a bit giddy showing him the landlord's Doberman ashes, the cabinets full of brass swords, Toby jugs and bric-a-brac antiques, the green velvet chaise longue over three hundred years old. 'Jesus, what kind of place is this, what the hell are you doing here?' The sunlight flared through the four windows making glossy crutches of white which he started to playfully maul. 'I spend my days in cahoots with the sea,' I told him, which was true. Listening to the callous smack of it in the mornings, soothing myself with the surging anger in the early evening when the lighthouse woke. I couldn't afford heating so lit the open fire most days. Fantasies about setting myself up as a prostitute at the house seemed ugly and irrelevant, but I imagined for a moment that he might be my first client driving through treacherous bends on the cliff road in furious hail to whinge about his wife being sent silk tights in the post by a stranger. That I would kneel in front of him and push my cold hands up through the hem of his trousers, clawing at the bunched hairs. Taking the full warm weight of his dick on my lips which I knew I was particularly good at. 'Nothing ever feels real for me,' I said. 'But this place is some wacky beautiful shit all the same. Makes me think I might be ready to die.' I went for a bath and returned with nothing on, which I never do. He knew not to stare, that I'd find that devious, intimidating. We lay on the Indian pile rug with the flames flicking their harsh yellow ink into the ether. How many women had done this, opened their legs for a lover in firelight down through the centuries, hoping it'd make a modest difference to the workings of love?

I tried to let them fall apart as wide as I could, but was foiled and obstructed, a faulty mussel shell. Slowly he slid two fingers in. I asked for more, asked him to make sure to remember me. 'Push it all in,' I said. 'Just ignore me if I cry.'

From: Ivan Campbell <666ni@yahoo.co.uk>
Sent: 11 June 2016 14:59
To: Rosie Dew
Subject: Re: Re: Re: Re: Those salt mines

I have it on very good authority that the salt mines at Kilroot were on a list of three final redoubt locations for the UK executive and some members of the monarchy. They are dry, a thousand feet down with vehicle access and could easily withstand a 1-megaton direct hit. Apparently in the 1970s food, medical supplies and weapons were stored there, but this was absolutely top secret and after Thatcher came to power for some odd reason they were taken off the list. Are you talking about an actual nuclear bunker? Was that on Twitter or are you properly stalking me you little weirdo!? It was one of those Mickey Mouse things that a guy restored, about the size of Father Ted's caravan. At one point there were fifteen hundred of them dotted around the UK, part of the government's scam to make the populace think an all-out Soviet attack was survivable (Protect & Survive hide under some doors bollocks). There was a public info film they used to show before Swap Shop and it scared the living crap out of me. That pip-pip-pip sound still spooks me even now. BTW, I'm doing an online course on black holes these days, dark energy and gravitational waves. Theoretical physics suggests we could survive passage into a rotating black hole. Now there's one hell of a ride, so keep looking out for the spinning ones.

June I find this amusing you bouncing emails back and forth talking away no problem all on for it all fucking sexy out slutty witch gung-ho then boomf nothing nada off I go and hide again when it suits me playing your poxy upswing downswing manic mind games dangerous fucking mind games do you ever learn? Push and push and push gush. Your cunt can't even fit a fucking cock properly it's all wrong up there whatever happened you how your bloke doesn't smash your fucking brain in with a claw hammer I'll never know wild horny affairs and why wouldn't he putting up with the dribbly mentally ill fucking drivel from you? My biggest regret was leaving you and Katie too quickly that night two hours later I woke wishing I'd fucked you from behind up on that big solid table in the kitchen baboon fucking after tying that mad bastard bitch to a chair to make her watch never shut up do you constantly fucking harping on you self-obsessed narcissistic cunt think we really wanted to ride YOU!? Marcus's email laughing at how you don't come can't come don't know how to come won't come imagine at your age even your G-spot has given up hope vagus nerve sloppy cervix crying in the dark feeling sorry for yourself finger stuck up looking to us like we owed you who gives a fuck? Ugly fat bastard wanker we were flying the motorway screwing gorgeous women not disgusting ugly dogs who can't spread 'em or who have trouble even getting up onto a bed for a good going over gorgeous women real women take it up the bum women screaming for more decent bodies great bodies gym sun beach ballerina beautiful whore bodies not fucking a pile of broken hips moles scars women men would stop and dribble over on the street wank over sweaty jocks sore knob smelly fingers fanny cry over better-looking versions of Kirsty Allsop in black halter-neck dresses that do little to cover huge fucking knockers with proper brown banging hard nipples not pink bird shit nipples like yours striking model blondes in black wet-look leggings and tight red tops to show off equally massive tits wonderful tall sexy shapely women who know how to carry it off who know how to cock tease and mean it not small squat hairy arse bitches in terrible PVC shit that they can't even put fucking on properly looking like a German MILF slut wagon arsehole basement gangbanger with lights turned out so ugly who'd want to shoot their load in that! Look at me me me me me me geebag good mind to drag you by the hair down the concrete steps drag you over to the Ranger's Club for all them hepped-up lads to piss and shit and cum all over you taking turns you vile bad make-up bitch oh I live by the sea look at me dumb Jane Austen wannabe fucking hogslut open your crooked yellow sticky out teeth fucking small mouth take it white worms whole load of white worms thick cream two lots choke bitch gurgle choke slap dripping down your chin cry your arse out on stinking feet sheets howling like a fucking child who needs the butt of that up your arse piss off roll over fat fuck die cripple cracked.

We meet in Jury's Inn on Parnell Street three years on. Him in a black linen suit and khaki T-shirt with meerkats popping their brazen heads out of an army tank. Me with a crimson chin from scratching too much in sleep. We hug awkwardly; polite bash of bones; he makes a pitiful attempt to finger a curling tongs effect into the back of my hair; stops when he feels me wince; we pigeon our way to the lifts. I can no longer remember how to negotiate his size or how to brush him with meaning. I push up on my toes to peck his cheek. He shoves his arms tight into the shoulder sockets. I hold on to his elbow. Two Americans in tweed blazers dangle brown leather suitcases and stare. A janitor whisks through with a brass trolley calling and waving to a high-heeled woman who's left a laptop asleep on a bed. It feels good that he's a stranger again. I am turned on by it. Turned on by knowing how much he can hurt me. I keep my head down in the lift while he looks up at the synthetic sky. Red circles on the lift buttons keep climbing. I have practiced what I want to say. I've read Freud. Got a better longer lingering understanding of the human condition (through yet another dead man). Sex hurts. I'm learning to drive. I've even read some good novels. People belonging to me have passed on. Others are refusing to. There's no harm in humiliation. No lasting injury at least. I fucking liked it. We learn best from when we mess up most. The humanity in that. Think about that. How do I explain that? Bring on the dancing chestnuts. Bring in the charming psychopaths. How does he not remember the woman who fell in love with the

Second Life avatar? A nurse from Carrickfergus. She stopped feeding her kids. They ran out of fish fingers. A vampire from Scotland. They got taken away from her. I had to go talk to her as one of his assignments. We didn't really make the most of our time. She came to meet me at the seafront. I've learnt so much since. Even the funny stuff. The man I slept with in London really did have too much girth. The big cock thing is a tedious lie. Felt like someone was trying to shove a caravan up between my thighs. Let's have a good laugh about that! Let's laugh about sex! Let's go for a drive! My guy sitting in a soft chair in the corner watching. All I could think of was Bart Simpson saying 'wiener' over and over. We strolled around London looking for a theatre show afterwards. Didn't have sex for at least two years. Dead people watching and all that. He shouldn't feel guilty for the way he spoke to me. The opposite. Where would it have all careered off to? He did me a favour. I deserved it. You did me a favour. I deserve it. Good to be made to feel lonely once in a while. How else do we ever get to feel properly alive? I touch myself when I think about it. How horrified it made me feel. My guy is having an affair with a TED Talks woman. He doesn't know I know. So much for the open relationship. A beautiful pixie with bony knees, huge eyes. So much for enduring honesty. He's too busy with his job to satisfy me anyhow. We could do it for just two hours a week. I know someone who'd lend us a room. A man in the arts who organises those kinds of parties. Starched collar orgies! All that talk of funding in between lashes. We could be strategic with our time. Treat it like therapy. Punch in sore silence. Take it far. I so deserve it. Get advice from other people. See where we land. The lift door opens and the waitress says, 'Sorry, no tables, but check back again in an hour.' Two window cleaners are suspended from rope outside. Alphabet spaghetti on aluminium glass. The sun lends a mean streak of purple. Glen says, 'Look, I can't be doing with the madness of Dublin, sorry, I'll leave you to it. I'm glad things worked out for you. I always knew they would.'

The Man Who Lived In A Tree

Rashi waited for his tormentors by the pissy park gates. Balloon faces from years on the gear; bodies so thin they could thread through gaps in garden gates all across the lit grid of suburbia. They mauled their way around in the limp hours hassling the likes of him trying to live a cloistered life. Most were just passing through the bend at Broadstone, heading on south towards the quays to score some scag. Or back down the crack in the road to the high rises. He wondered how they'd managed to spot him in the first place. For two months, four days and a couple of lean hours, he'd peeled off the city pathways entirely, heading up an old willow tree beside Brannigans pub and the Odlums flour factory that looked like a Sealink ferry flopped on its side.

'Story, bud!?' they'd shout up at him, in unison. 'Story?'

'The bleeding head on ye, did ye get that in a charity shop mate, did ye?'

'Here, Isaac Newton, throw us down a few light bulbs.'

'Any gorgeous birds up there?'

His home was planted on a small patch of avocado grass on the bend where the houses tattletaled behind a hairy park. To the front some redbrick council flats (mostly boarded up). At the side the bulk of bus station with its parked army poking out above a beanstalk wall now being smashed up to accommodate the Luas line extension. In the squiggle of high branches he laid out a single-plank bed using pilfered clothing full of cotton wool to keep him snug. On lower branches he flung clothes, photographs, a leather satchel his father used when he was a revenue collector, a tablecloth stolen from the Maldron Hotel, letters from his mother, EuroShop toolkits, grilled crisp bags, a lifelong collection of medals. Lying crabways he'd watch the locals paint their lungs russet outside the pub, crowing about monies owed and goods stowed. On his back staring up between the crown and the treetop: 100,000,000,000,000,000,000,000 overcooked stars that seemed to have a lot in common with him. When he closed his eyes he was able to muster up Lorna in their bedsit in Camden. Pirouetting across the floor to the swampy arias of Kate Bush. Goading him about reconstituted spuds they were about to have for dinner again. 'One, two or ten?' she'd ask, cocking her leg behind her in a kind of chef-jest. 'They taste of nothing but water! What say you snuggle head, are you a hungry boy?'

For an entire summer they'd lived on tinned potatoes, kidney beans at 19p a tin and Fray Bentos pies. She was taking a course in Contemporary Dance for Performance at a small amateur getup in North London and liked to prance about in the evenings in her sky-blue knickers and guipure lace bra, cooking up the same leaden fare on the one-ring hob over and over. He adored her milky boobs and olive eyes, her animal cackle and the fact she could only fuck with her clothes partially on because she was so 'County Wexford shy'. On those smoky summer nights in 1988, he sprinted all the way from the building site in Chalk Farm in the still sweltering glare of evening to pin her to the bed for as many hours as he could. She found it impossible to look at him straight on. He'd stretch her elfin hands behind to the bed bars. Jammed like a butterfly, she'd give in, rooted in pleasure, squealing to the ceiling plaster and scarlet sky out above. 'Give it to me again,' she'd say. 'Push inside deep as you can.' He'd kiss and lick the sweat off her for ages. He would've sucked her up whole through a straw if he could. Afterwards they'd watch arthouse films, before flopping into repose in the single bed, wrapped like burritos. His work of lugging bricks and metal poles starting up again as early as 5 a.m. The foremen were all Irish, which planted the first kernel for visiting Ireland one day. Lorna talked about it a lot. She always stuck a small bunch of black grapes in his jacket pocket so he'd have something healthy to eat on the move. They took care of each other.

It was a good few weeks before the tree spoke to him. Speckles of information at first: age (169 years); classification: Grey Willow; planting date (as yet unknown, same too for exactly how he got in the ground); how he loved the rain and sodden soil beneath him; the oval-shaped leaves that tickled all year round; his greyish green fleece-like belly; sawflies, aphids, caterpillars and leaf beetles that populated his arms and legs since the primary days; things he'd seen and witnessed: famine, Republican marches, car crashes, building booms, child rape, dog snatches, stabbings, carnivals, Christmas celebrations, guided tours, industrial strikes, Luftwaffe raids, surreptitious deals beneath his bough when the chickpea moon was at full-flourish.

'My ancestors are the Salicaceae from China. Scientific name: *Salix cinerea subsp*. Oleifolia. Often known to botanic know-it-alls as "common sallow". We're better settled next to lakes or ponds but the tempestuous weather here does me fine my friend. How long do you hope to hang around? I'd like to tell you that you're the first though I did have a malodorous old bag lady grow into my branches back in 1938, a year before the War broke out. Her husband a right panhandler all been told. Had her beaten to a pulp most nights until she ran away.'

Rashi completely ignored him at first. After a few days he'd spew back a 'piss off' or 'fuck up', shaking Willow's rusty veins until some of his own oddities fell onto the soggy ground. 'Is me being here dragging you down?' he asked Willow one Saturday afternoon when he felt he could no longer resist the voice. The fine old gentleman tree assured him all was grand and peachy as long as he didn't spill chemicals on him or cut into branches with sharp objects.

'A chap of wine hair persuasion once considered it somewhat a witty thing to splosh superglue on some of my lower branches. I made sure to remember. Did him a disfavour next time he stuck his bony posterior at my trunk.'

'What did you do?'

'Well if you recall, Shakespeare's Ophelia drowned close to a willow, didn't she?' He refused to elaborate but kept grinning. A bit imbecilic, Rashi thought. Beneath his foliage being eaten by caterpillars, moths and a very regal purple emperor butterfly, he smiled like a monkey with a new banana. Willow greased him with prudent tips from the silver felt of his under-leaves on the art of being indistinguishable, the best time of day to head off scavenging for food or other sundries he might need. All manner of kind advice he never expected from anyone anymore under any circumstances.

'You need to take care around here, keep one eye brewing at all times,' Willow cautioned. 'The escalation of drugs around and about is nothing short of heart-stopping. Marauding gangs hawking their trade in the all-encompassing daylight, brash as you like.'

Rashi had seen it with his own inky eyeballs. Knackbags dropping off stacks of cash and sports bags stuffed with what could be handguns. Nippers from the flats flailing in the grip of chemico-crash. One of them, a scaldy maggot of just fifteen, was venerated for biting off a security guard's ear outside McGowans where horny nurses went sniffing for prison officer husbands on Wednesdays. It was all drink, drugs, litter, loss, random violence and mayhem, according to Willow.

'Residents have a right pain in their you-know-what,' he explained. 'Complaining 24/7 there's nowhere safe for their uncouth youths to kick a ball.'

By early evening he gathered his bob-bits from under the scrag of bushes to put back up the tree. Across the way Lower Dominick Street was beetling alive. Plywood apartments with artificial fireplaces and thermofoil kitchens emptying residents out through electronic gates in search of something to do. He'd lived up that stink of road before. Prostituted himself when his mother flew over from Loharu Tehsil to compost him for good. It wasn't just about the money – he needed cash when the boom work dried up – it was principally about punishment. He could do nothing but guzzle himself into more torpor after Lorna's death; hating himself for being unable to stop it. 'You can't stick fast in this horrible country destroying yourself bachcha, bringing shame down on us, not caring a damn,' his mother whined. 'You're disgracing the family, disrespecting yourself, bruising me.' He understood. She'd witnessed his father do it for a bucket of years.

His drinking got way out of hand even when himself and Lorna were still in the vice-grip of idolatry. 'It can't be helped, petal,' he told her. 'You're obliged to go for drinks if you want to pipe work for the following week … they give priority to the men who stay on after hours.' He had come home to catch her in tears. Snotting inconsolably in her Victorian drawers and tap pants he bought in a vintage shop in Islington for a crazy £40, equivalent to one week's rent. It wasn't even her birthday but he loved her so perfectly he couldn't resist witnessing that lick of bliss on her face. 'You're losing yourself mohabbat,' she replied. Her pet name for him in Hindi, *love*. 'I'm starting to think I don't know the real you anymore.' It made him heavy with misery when she spouted such awful melancholia. He couldn't bear the idea of ever being without her. Life would be a half life minus her whirling around giddy inside it. 'It's only a few pints of Guinness, it's not like you don't enjoy a drink yourself.' It was a different thing to sup together all happy out, she felt, than to come home drooling and dripping, smelling terrible. Too late to do fun stuff like they used to when they were buddy-buddy in the cramped bedsit they felt so lucky to get. A lot of landlords didn't tolerate cohabiting couples and especially mixed-race cohabiting couples. He didn't stop drinking after work because he wasn't able to. Towards the end of her first year, Lorna started hanging out more with her dance troupe of posh gits and retro quacks after practice sessions. Smoking joints at music gigs in the Engine Room or the Lock Tavern. When he'd arrive late drunk as a skunk song with a carryout of Carlsberg Special Brew under his drizzly armpit, her friends sneered, gazing into the hinterland of makeshift stage. Britpop band Blur hung out in these drink dens before they became properly famous. The drummer had a *grá* for Lorna which made Rashi more than mad. 'If you want to go there, then go there,' he said. The sinkhole look on her face.

'You missed the busybodies when you were off gallivanting earlier,' Willow informed him. 'Talking about serving an eviction notice on me for you. They are a canker my friend.'

'There's nothing illegal about me being here. Nada. Not a thing they can do.'

He'd looked it up in the National Library, the new-fangled anti-loitering laws. There was only mention of being firmly on the ground, outside ATMs. Beggars holding out cupped hands to collect coins. Roma on roundabouts. Wizened women holding newborns up like placenta-covered puppies. Laws so bygone that statute books still insisted you carry a bale of hay with you to feed your method of transportation. No one could tell him he was doing anything wrong. Dublin City Council itself was not aware of any deeds for the tree.

'A woolly social worker with them, dressed in pink, blathering on about the Mental Health Act,' Willow said. Rashi thought he could hear him snickering but he couldn't be certain.

'Who you talking to?' one of the local scuzzers roared over. A pallet of new eighteen-year-olds had just qualified for drinking in Brannigans, spilling out every night to abuse him on their short hop home.

'Spanner brain, I'm talking to you, who you yacking at?'

'Give them whatsfor,' Willow advised. 'Or there'll be no let up. I wouldn't put it past them to take a blowtorch to my tired old legs. Have you seen the new burl on my back there? It's really unsightly ...'

Rashi would never answer them back. What was the point?

'Hey! Charlie Chapati, do us up an aul filthy kebab!'

Chucking blobs of wet toilet roll. Hurling them in the dark. Not letting up until scores of soaking splotches stuck to Willow and him like cockleburrs.

'Grab hold of that there,' one of them instructed his muscle mate in a torn combat jacket. Pissing their cacks laughing. Eight or nine of them yanking a garden hose from around the side of the pub over onto the lonesome patch where Willow stood majestic as the great High King Lóegaire mac Néill, fierce and pagan. They pulled and hauled and slapped it into position, before turning on the outdoor tap full blast. Some of them were so drunk they began to wiggle and weave under the weight. 'Stall the ball!' they shouted. 'Gerra proper grip on it.'

'Why are they doing this to me?' Rashi asked, eyes yellow as a frog's belly. 'What have I ever done on them, on anyone?'

'Leave the poor fucker alone,' the barman told them. 'Stop the fucking messing or you won't get served, deyezhearme?'

'Cool the beans, we're just giving him a power shower for his little gaff up there.'

'You must admit, they are rather buoyant with rolling punches,' Willow chuckled.

'Yamadev and Shanidev will punish the likes of them for their wickedness,' he told Willow.

'Hmmm, indeed, but we don't do those exotic gods here. Just that wearisome fellow with the beard and pretty dress who guzzles wine and sports a tremendously sexy foot fetish.'

He was beginning to think he'd picked the wrong temple to rest up in and that Willow was a bit of a smart alec who liked to mess him around. Thinking about it properly he'd need a camouflaged platform a hundred feet off the ground, possibly a Douglas fir in the Botanic Gardens, to stay out of harm's way. Parnell Street was rough when he was holed up there for a few months outside Cineworld, but this was steadily getting worse. Back then the congeries of German men on 'culture holidays' looking for a group jiggle outside the sports bar left him alone. As did the brawny truckers with a furtive hunger they preferred their A-line wives not know about. Businessmen who needed to be sucked off before bi-monthly stock flotations. Whores on high heels hunting horny punters. Libertine hipsters and their flowery frock girlfriends. None of those types paid him any heed. There was so much sex on the streets after hours. Quick fumbling hasty half fucks. Legs plastered against pebbled walls. Devil-may-care moans. It didn't bother him much. Not like the spiteful violence others helped themselves to before hopping into late-night taxis. He'd often get a quick kick or a wallop after 2 a.m. Cans of half-supped lager lobbed at his head. Needle jammed in the back of his thigh he never got checked out because he didn't have a medical card. Two winters in he'd been roughed up too many times and found himself back out on concrete, living at the back of a restaurant beside a humming fan. There was always food in the laneways, a vortex of throwaway. Some of the foreign workers left out dregs for him after the clean-up of nightshift spillage. Bits of sloppy taco, jerk chicken, wild wilted spinach and other khaki leaves plucked from the roadsides of Wicklow and Meath for wannabe Michelin stars.

'Take it out here and be good to it,' the only friend he ever met before Willow, Dhudha, would say, passing out cardboard plates through the ventilation hole. He had come all the way from Uttar Pradesh where hunter-gatherers first lived in wood huts along sluggish rivers of the Bhabhar. Rashi had visited there himself for a family wedding as a small boy. Mesmerised by the buzz of two hundred million voices and monsoons emptying from its skies. Dhudha's English was hilariously bad and nothing he emitted made sense. 'My boss says you are the baggabond! He kill me if he knew I food you!'

Sometime in 2012, the Somali dealers moved in around the laneways of Parnell Street, pegging their powders to the nostril-famished. Restaurants closed down because of racketeering. He never saw Dhudha again but dreamt he was back in India in a jam-packed town selling clunky wooden toys to foreign children on the side of a hill. Spending afternoons pointing his donkey-skin feet into the marmalade sunshine. Three people were done with blades in these laneways. Two men pretty much like him hospitalised from beatings that left them with sixteen broken bones between them. It was a catwalk of mêlée – not a ruddy-faced Garda in sight – so once again he moved to the porch of a banana warehouse at the back of the Four Courts. Later, he dragged himself and his belongings up towards Broadstone to a bandstand in Temple Gardens where he sang out loud on bitterly cold days.

'You're better off here even if you do get drenched by those rascals,' Willow told him. 'I'll keep watch in case they crawl back over. Try to get some sleep my friend. *Is iad gáire maith agus codladh fada an dá leigheas is fearr ar rud ar bith.'*

He hated when Willow spoke to him *as Gaeilge*. Another thing he'd started doing in recent weeks to frustrate him. How could Rashi intervene if the pub dipsos did more than goad or spray him with water next time? There was a dull feeling in his heart. The kind he felt the last time Lorna skipped out the door in 1989. A seeping dread he couldn't justify. Parked in the Monarch with four others from the building site after work when the police came hoofing around looking for him. 'You need to come with us,' they said. Outside he resisted for a moment until they told him in swarthy tones, no no, he'd have to go with them. He really had to go. Now. It had started to spit rain. Steel grey of spring sky squalling down on top of him. Get your jacket. Get your things. They offered him a ham sandwich from a vending machine at the station in Kentish Town and a milky coffee. One of the lady officers was sheathed in peroxide and looked like Myra Hindley. They'd already spoken to the foreman Johnny. Did Lorna work part time? Was she seeing anyone else? Was there a reason she might be wandering around Farringdon Road so late? It was a good bit away from the dance school. Had she been followed before? Were there any tenants in the house that seemed a bit odd? Her crimson pointe pumps shoes pressed up against the cupboard when he got home. Half erect as if they still had tiny feet pushed deep into them waiting for Tchaikovsky to give the nod.

At night Rashi mummified himself in rope and ribbons to the upper branches so he wouldn't fall off. The plank bed was hard as destiny and any attempt at bedding just made it worse with the perpetual rain showers. Willow serenaded him with really annoying lullabies too, as if he was four years old. *You must love me Diddle Diddle cause I love you, I heard one say Diddle Diddle, Once I came hither, That you and I Diddle Diddle must lie together.*

'Come out Tarzan ye mad yoke!' one of the men from the pub shouted over.

He woke to a big kerfuffle below. Willow teasing him downwards with the aid of his hairiest branches, into the arms of a fluffy social worker with a padded jacket and silly smile.

'Hello!' she said, casually. 'We'd really like to help. This is so hard on you here, with the weather getting worse. We may have a solution.'

'A Bachelor in the Fine Art of Interfering, the likes of her,' Willow said, shaking coins from the upper branches onto the Guard and the barman who were mooching around like lemons. 'Throw her a Wonderland quote: when you can't look on the bright side I'll sit with you in the dark. Tell her to go hassle some single mothers who can't cope.'

'What has happened here mohabbat?' Lorna asked. She wasn't being judgemental, more like softly concerned. Her pale face scrubbed with sadness. 'This is a terrible day.' She'd only come to him twice in all the years since. Once on a ferry bound for Brittany when a British soldier on leave from Afghanistan threatened to throw Rashi overboard for stealing his seat in the cinema lounge. Another time when he was having a fling with the Greek yoga teacher he visited in Gerakas to see the loggerhead turtles. They tried to make love on the beach out of sight of the other tourists but he kept seeing Lorna. She was standing not far off, holding a bunch of wildflowers, watching them. He lost his nerve after that.

The pot-bellied Guard began orating from a clipboard some lackey or other handed him. 'In accordance with section 16(h) of the Residential Tenancies Act 2004 you are obliged not to behave within the above dwelling, or in the vicinity of it, in a way that is anti-social ...'

'Fuck up!' Rashi said. 'I'm not renting this tree. I am a free man!'

'It's time now,' the social worker said in a low voice, reaching her hand out like a zoo handler.

He was exhausted running away for a living. Worn out by strangers badgering and hassling, of aimless voices following, shadows prickling.

'Get off the grass ye mentler!' 'Stop scaring the kids!' Gaggle of women from the flats in Penney's pyjamas over-populated with cuddly bears and climbing cats. 'You're a smelly bollix!'

A reporter from the *Evening Herald* fiddled with a digital recorder. He wanted to interview Rashi about what a nation of racists Ireland had become. Did he have any opinions on Brexit? Was he homeless out of choice? Was he making some sort of political statement?

'I want to be left alone,' he told him. 'All I desire in the world is a good night's sleep.'

Some of the women became agitated when they saw the Garda mauling Rashi roughly.

'There's real criminals over in the pub but they might be too scary for ye?'

'Haven't you got tax discs to check out on the road there?'

It was not the end Rashi often dreamt about. He would just be about to doze off, resting his tender neck on a gnarl for the night. Faint buzz of white noise approaching. He'd be dosed up on Bluegreen shots. Glops of Goldschläger, gobs of Guinness. Other leftovers he ritually collected from sticky tables as last orders rang out, poured into a polythene beaker. The gang at the park gates hunching up and over. Banging the railings with sticks and bars, jokes and jars. Making their way onto his sacred mandir of grass.

'Kick the living shite out of the fucker, the seagulls will scoff his brains by morning.'

In front of him Lorna's dead legs doing a bunny hop. Her sapphire blue ballet dress with the white tutu she'd spent six months saving like mad for. Formerly hung in all kinds of strange twists and inclines from the self-adhesive wall knobs meant for tea towels. 'I know it's childish,' she'd said. 'But I need to feast my eyes on it as soon as I wake in the morning.' Willow in an ungovernable rage, spurting sap in every direction, submerging half a dozen scallywags beneath the spongy ground. But even that wouldn't stop the tormentors. They'd disco on Rashi's entrails when he lay silent and subdued, on and on until wholly broken.

'There on the willow trees, we hung up our harps,' Willow whispered to Rashi as his head was pressed down into the back of the Garda car. 'It's a sad day to witness such a fine fellow being hauled off to the madhouse.' Rashi stared out at the last friend he'd ever have on free land and wondered in earnest if he'd ever cared about him at all. He seemed to be bootlegging in the breeze, flinging branches about, entangled in celebration. It was not a coincidence that he chose him as a companion. Willow was riddled with black canker and didn't have long to live. Rashi had hoped they'd sink down into the glum earth together. Like on the Indonesian island Tana Toraja, where, if a baby dies before it starts teething, the family cuts a hole in a tree and places the dead child inside. The tree regrows around the baby and absorbs it. Rain poured down as the car slid off, staining the pathways with silvery tears. Willow shouted after him, 'Salicylic acid from my leaves is used to manufacture aspirin, remember that, won't you? It may turn up on a quiz one day.'

Natterbean

He knew he smelt like a sardine but that's what Polish beer does to a man on a low wage. With names like Tatra, Tyskie, and Żywiec, he may as well have been downing fermented donkey piss the night before. The smug knotty face on the bent cop who ran the off license on a privately paid-for unflappable hip made him madder than a hacksaw. To top it off he woke to Gina screaming blue butchery as he forgot the green lentils again – on a wholefood buzz since her arse went all weather balloon – he still hadn't got around to sorting out the monkey business with her. Burrowing in his chest hair for six torturous weeks. But today it was the thoughts of Natterbeans that was pushing him comprehensively into the dark place. Swarming the roads and cycle lanes. Using his waxed bonnet at traffic lights as a fat walking stick to get them to where they didn't remember they had to go on the other side. If he'd half a brain or a quarter of a heart he'd feel sorry for the fuckers, but they were a type of celestial cabbage he loathed. When he passed Fanagans Funeral Home with the overflowing bottle bins slumped at its gates, bits of torn brown tights flying from the tangled railings of an aulone's wet dream, one of them hopped in all lickety-spit.

'Alright bro! You and me are mates aren't we? Yer nor gonna give me no jip cos I'm having a fuck of a day like? I'll pay ye goodo, yeah. I'll see ye alright when I get me glasses as me old ma used to say but I never really knew what she meant. Ma's are stone fucking mad aren't they? You know what I'm gerrin' at, don't ye? I'll shut me trap now, we'll probably get there quicker. Isn't that the way bud? You from around here?'

'Where are we off to?' he asked. Knowing that to politely remove the plank from the back seat after he'd already pressed the fare button would be undue hassle. 'Just tell me where we're heading to so we can make a move.' The roads ahead slippy and slimy. He'd have to drive slow and meticulously, sunk stupid in Natterbean's backdoor trots splattering from his gob.

'Well I tell ye what, I'm natterbean up at the clinic and they was fucking me around cos they says I ain't got a prescription or that I did have a yokedymadoo in anyways but I don't no more so I've to head to this other gaff up around Meath Street and talk to Mr Doherty who'll sort me out at another clinic till the Finglas one get word of where their prescription went to … One hand doesn't know who's scratching the nebs of the other … bunch of bleeding jokers.'

'Look, where are we going to?' he asked again. Not so politely this time, adding that he wanted to see the cash. 'Out with the spondoolies, I need to know if you can sort the fare.'

'Stall the ball there bud. Don't be going all Donald Trump on me. Think I'm just another dopey trackie don't ye? But here, c'mere, I'm natterbean up at the cash machine so we're good to wangle. I'm not fucking dense. I can answer most questions on *The Chase*. Do ye watch dat, do ye? Fucking love that programme. Gas the way greedy bolloxes say they're going to buy a gaff, then they go home with fuck all when them fat chasers ram them up the hole.'

He'd been stung too many times lately by the likes of him. The last Natterbean, he had to reef him back into the car through the front window by the scruff. So far gone, so wasted, so emaciated, he would've been able to do a runner through a cat flap if he'd had his jimminy bits about him. That particular night he drove like a gazelle with a rocket up its shitepipe, through the Port Tunnel, up past the airport. Out into the spuds and strawberries-for-sale countryside with its vulgar pretend Tudor houses and Breaded Chicken Breast With Pineapple pubs. Dumping him in a field without his Nikes or bubble down jacket. A few hard farewell slaps. Took his social welfare and medical cards just so he'd forget forever who he was supposed to be. Left him there at the hem of humanity for the dawn to deal with.

'It's nice to be nice, you know? Don't be all rough bud like one of them bleeding leg breakers. Didn't I tell ye we were going up as far as Meath Street. I'm natterbean in two Jo Maxis and they were like, the same as that. I've plenty of paper on me so I have. I'll give ye extra if ye wait for us. I'll give ye a tenner up front now, alright bud, even though yezer clock only says a fiver so far, how's that for a bargain bucket?'

'Do me a favour,' he said, this time pulling the taxi over to the side of the road before they headed further into the cesspit. 'Will ye try to shut your hoop on the way? I can't concentrate if someone's nattering constantly. Trying to keep me mincers on the traffic. Nothing personal. I'm sure you're a nice fella, blah blah blah. But we'll get on much better if we can get there as quickly and as peacefully as we can.'

He adjusted the mirror to take a closer look. Natterbean had the same mushroom pallor and knee-jerkiness as the others, but with a thin pointy face that was extra alert. Morning fox in an industrial estate looking for crane flies. His uneven shoulders and busted nose were typical. Teeth yellow as corn on the cob. Stinking of Lynx over dirt and cherry bubblegum. As he drove past Glasnevin Cemetery, he was reminded of the tour guide who supped the pints in his local boozer. He'd be beating on about how the bodies of the rich were interred in fancy private tombs but in recent times Natterbeans were breaking in in the dead of night pricking themselves and the ghosts with heroin needles. The ornamental pathways planted with Lebanon cedar, red sequoia, oak, beech and yew, were spattered with blood and empty Tayto bags. Soon they'd be in sight of the quays and he'd be rid of him, circling back to grab sure-fire fares from the airport.

'Yeah yeah yeah yeah, what did I fucking tell ye? He's a poxy messer. Fucking headwreck. Don't be minding him. Total spacer.' Whining into his blower. 'I'm natterbean up there with Natalie this morning and she says it's sorted. I've to go here first on a message, gizza buzz back in an hour.'

He was glaring at the mobile, pressing on the buttons like a reflexology tosspot would on a scabby foot. 'Here, bud, will ye pull over there for a sec. There's me old homey at the corner, I owe him a note.'

Homey was a fat man on one leg with a squeegee of green hair you could wash a pile of dishes with. He could hear the Honda 50 drawl of both their voice boxes building up at breakneck speed into an ambulance siren, 'warrrhhh warrrrhhh warrrrh warrrr', before he jumped back in the car again. Better not be messing him around. The meter was up to €14 already. He wasn't about to bring him on a round-trip of inner city Dublin dealers in creepy car parks and lurid laneways strewn with needles, plastic cartons, banana skins, blood-soaked knickers. The one yesterday, a good-looking dolly, had the wool rightly pulled, taking him to five different chemists for 'phy' while robbing them of expensive wrinkle cream.

'I'm only trying to make an honest living like you are,' she'd said, jumping back into his car. 'I'm natterbean in prison four times already and I'll never go back, so relax the cacks.'

His reg was taken on CCTV and traced. He had to call into the Guards and explain himself. It's not his job to ask questions as long as the punter pays up, but he got a fine from the carriage office regardless.

'Can ye turn down here for a minute bud,' he said when they hit the grey bulk of Christchurch. 'There's me mate Bottler, just want to say howayea. His missus had a sprog a few weeks back. They'd to sew up her piss bag an all, she's in an awful state.'

Bottler staggered out of a doorway looking like a grade-A psycho who'd crack your toes off and use them as ear plugs for nights he was slumped under the motorway bridge unable to crawl to anywhere else. Natterbean gave him a man slap on the shoulder and limped his way back to the car.

'That fella looks like a bit of a header if you don't mind me saying.' He wanted to draw his attention to the clock. 'Just letting you know with the few stops already, it's up to €22 now.'

'No bother bud,' he said. 'Here's another Lady Godiva. I'll give ye the rest when we get there. He used to be a brilliant house breaker, but the Hungarians have it wrapped up so they do. Put fucking broken glass outside bedroom doors. If ye hear clatter in the middle of the night, right, ye smash yer feet right up if ye gander to see what's going down. Filthy stuff that is. We never did nothing like that. Always straight in and out. It's not on. Some poor oldie prick cutting his feet to ribbons. You don't do shit like that but the Hungarians and Poles are bonkers. No bleeding respect.'

At the corner of Meath Street and Engine Alley a red hoodie made a run for the window. 'There ye are ye mad cunt!' he roared in. 'I'm natterbean talking about you to Skittles and the lads!' He held onto the boot as the lights turned green, falling over on his arse and rolling towards the drain. Natterbean was punching more digits on his mobile as the chemist came into view. He thought of Gina and her constant trips to McCabe's for fake tan. Except she'd gotten the mangy Egyptian one, looked like runny dog shite slipping down her pins. It didn't strike him as odd at the time either that she'd started getting her fanny waxed into a Brazilian landing strip, whatever the bejaysisfuck that was, saying that it stopped her getting itchy. 'It's €28 on the clock, I'll need paying as soon as you come out.'

He'd accidentally seen her Tinder chat a few weeks before. Gina left her pink iPhone in the newly built utility room thrown on top of some dirty duvet covers ironically enough – he hadn't even heard of dating apps for phones – a kind of Hailo for getting your hole. It might've only been a series of narks with this Paul but he doubted it. She was a right goer when she could be arsed putting it out. Up to three times a day when they met first. His knob the colour of a pit bull's nose. 'Bonobo' he'd called her. Always wanting it rough from behind. Hurt like fuck to know she could've been that lonely or desperate after twenty-two years. He'd decided not to tell her he knew but the knowing had done his snot in. Didn't sit pretty thinking what he could do to her if she continued messing him around. He could harm her so easily. Breaking her neck like a Brazil nut. Pushing her down the stairs when she was doing her aulone's trick of hauling two baskets of washing. Sticking ethylene glycol in her skinny mint hot chocolate to fuck up her kidneys. Now this knucklehead of a Natterbean was bashing digits just like she does with Candy Crush when she wakes in the mornings full of beans whiffing of boiled mackerel. There was probably a junkie app as well. Swaying thumb tacks on Google Maps for those desperate for a hit.

'You can pay me what you owe and get out of the car.'

'Don't be freaking the beak,' he said. 'Jaysis I'm natterbean in a queue the size of a black man's mickey. Fucking mayhem in there! They're making everyone down it in front of the nurses on account of wackos keeping it in their gobs. They do be spitting the phy out into plastic cups to sell outside. Here's a thirty spot. I need one more Cheesy Quaver over in Ringsend.'

Is this what she'd been doing too, sending him off on 'little jobs' as she called them? All over the grid while she got herself nice and slinky and reeking of Beyoncé Heat upstairs. Cut-price curtains in Debenhams. A parasol in Woodies. Under-the-bed shoe boxes from a boutique in Louth when they have them in Clearwater for a tenner … while yer man was messing with her plumbing controls at home? Playing with her faucets, bursting her storm drain. Her in some lace corset or other he hadn't seen or noticed from years ago. He wondered if any of the neighbours noticed him sidling up the driveway or if he had the smarts to park around the corner and stroll around casually. Grabbing Gina's tits in the hall. Shoving his hand up her skirt and calling her a dirty slut. He imagined himself around the back on the decking looking through the kitchen window down into the hall. Grabbing a baseball bat from the shed. Tearing through the door, zapping the fucker with one huge belt so his head split like a melon. Her screaming, leg still cocked, about to take him deep up the fandora. He liked the idea of making her clean his blood afterwards. Making sure she took her knickers off first. He'd sniff the crotch while he watched her swipe with the J-cloth, not even near spongy enough to soak up the clots. Crying like a zany bag at a pope's funeral. 'Wait until you see what I'm going to do with you next.'

'Are you dealing skank and using me as a muppet to drive you around?' he barked at Natterbean, who was, once again, slapping the shit out of his mobile phone.

'No way, no way, I'm no scummer, not like that, no way.'

He could see him now in the mirror pulling at a sausage shape in his crotch. He'd heard about heroin making them extra fertile and methadone making ye mad horny. Endless cycle of new drugs and new bellies full of babies. To think that him and Gina planned their kid right from when her ovaries were steaming. Up to the Camengo Lollipops & Animals wallpaper he'd ordered from France as a surprise after she'd done the big heave-ho. Didn't even wet the baby's head so he'd be there, bolder soldier by her side. Waited till the stitches healed to let her home in his taxi laced with cerise balloons chasing all three of them through the cobbles of Dublin. 'I'll suck the snot out of her hooter if I have to,' he promised Gina. 'When she gets on a bit I'll collect her in the work limo from school so she'll feel like a rap princess at her first gig down the O2.'

Natterbean pulled out a wad of notes, spilling a bundle over his feet. At least a couple of grand. A mate of his, Breezer, a real good spud, a dad, a brother, a footballer an' all before he kicked into the smack, was gonna get it in the head tonight from a knackbag worse than the Nidge. Wasn't even an IOU involved in this one, no. Refused to put lead in the head of another junkie who rode one of the dealer's pole tarts. Like he was an innocent fucker this bloke. Only got into the skank when his Ma died of tit cancer leaving him to look after six youngfellas, cooked his head big time. That's where they were heading now. He'd done a dip around to get him on the boat to Britland. 'I'll give ye a hundred to collect him at Ringsend and bring him safe to the boat in East Wall. We gorra deal bud?'

He wasn't expecting anything like this from the likes of that. 'What age is his nipper? Look, it's no problem, no harm to help a bloke out in a proper jam. This town is gone rough as a nun's moustache.'

'Son is eight, lives out of his ankles, you never see them apart, follows him around the town like a bleeding shadow, he's gutted so he is, poor cunt.'

Gina's bloke probably had a little bollox the same age. When he took his regular beached whale politician who smelt of egg mayonnaise from the Dáil up to the Blackrock Clinic to get the jab in her swollen gam, he'd squat outside with the engine off thinking of where the brat might go to school. Shifting up to the bushes near the gates. 'Here d'ye want these Pringles, I'm stuffed stupid, g'wan there's more than half left.' The greedy twit would stroll straight over, a thick fuck like his Da, trusting as the days goes by. He'd grab his small head, ramming the window closed on his snotter, hearing his high-pitched scream. Pulling the fucker's ears, giving him a few hard smacks. 'Tell your dirty aulfella that's what he gets for porking my wife.' Watching him in the mirror as he drove off, spinning on the path, an upside-down beetle.

Eyes wide open when they reached the docks. It wasn't that long since Nulty had his licence swiped and car impounded by Special Branch for helping Cocaine Crispin drop off a load set for the UK jog into Europe. Matters piggery shite if the cops know you're just a cog. More likely to go after the deputies than the mofos who can afford water wheels and brass dragons outside big dirty gaffs in Meath and Kildare. Nulty's missus shut the door and kept on power walking when he could no longer pay the mortgage. Never got over it, though he got back on track as a security guard after. 'That's it for me,' he told the lads in the Come On Inn. 'No more fish in the fryer when ye marry your first and pray she'll be the last. I wouldn't know what to do with a new bitch's wet bits. I'd fucking brown meself.'

The docks had a sheeny buzz since they'd done them all up on Fine Fáil chips. No more rust bunks sitting on giant metal plinths. Through civil wars and world wars and the IRA's gun-running gobshites on the run from themselves, they'd all hid down here, heads low. First batches of heroin were holed up in derelict warehouses full of pigeons. Prozzies from Eastern Europe were brought in through the sea gates. Young lives spent sucking on office peckers dreaming of getting out in a footballer's convertible before being shot in the head as a favour to a crack baron in Cabra for a write-off of a few quid or other. He could imagine the scrawny famine families dressed in linen sacks carrying malnourished mites onto ships here. Mooching back through history to see Gina and yer man up on deck staring down with grotto faces hoping for a fresh start in New York. Knowing they'd never be back again but being sure they'd starve to death on the way. He'd like to throw her back to the roaring famine and shove a pile of typhus down her gullet for good measure. Not in a million fucking years did he think she'd put out for anyone other than him. That had been the Majorca promise. Nothing but the egg smell of seaweed had stayed the same since those rotten times. There was even an apartment block now in the shape of a cruise liner for those twats that worked in Google and the likes. At night you could see the neon fish swimming up their walls as far out as Howth.

'There's the cunt there!' Natterbean said, pointing to a bloke in a grey duffel coat. Slumped up against a wet wall with black anchor chains, arguing with a seagull. 'Breezer, over here, c'mere, ye fucking queer!' He froghopped before the car had properly stopped. They wobbled towards each other. Slap slap, mind yerself, where's me gym bag, take care, no you take care, I'll take care, but will you take care, let us know. Stay under wraps until he heard of them getting de chop. All of them ones ended up sucking fat worms before they were thirty.

The way Breezer hugged yer man as if he was a warm marshmallow. Never seen anything like it. Sad bastard would be on the ferry in an hour thinking of his nipper he'd never fudge eyes on again. 'I need a hundred now before we go further,' he told Natterbean when he slumped back in. 'The clock's been off over an hour.' He drove slowly, snakily, ignoring the fact that he was crying. Junkies don't cry, he thought. They wouldn't know what it meant. He'd looked at the two bozos clouting about in the wind and felt in his guts they'd end up on the shite side of fate no matter how much they scrambled to look after themselves. Him and Gina hadn't done too bad all been told. They were on top of the bills, even with the insurance hikes on the motor in the last year. They always managed a big sloppy carvery on a Sunday. Got out for at least a few riproars in the month. Always made sure they had a right laugh. Sure hadn't he done a few slappers when they didn't have the dosh, instead of taking them to the Guards for the proper fare. Banged them over the leopard-fur front seats without giving Gina a thought. He tried not to think of that too much. Men had different needs to birds but it didn't have to mean anything sinister. Gave her at least two holidays a year, taking Cindy to Disneyland Paris for her sixth birthday, Gina begged him for months. She wanted for nothing and he said fuck all when she got the paint slopper in every Christmas to magic the walls cacky green.

No matter what she'd be moaning the toss when he got back. Ye forgot this, ye didn't pick up that. Didn't he get a right laugh out of her nagging him with her eyes going all big and hyper and mad? 'Where's me poxy lentils? Didn't I say no matter what bring me back the green lentils.' He'd be in no mood for a long ear-lashing with the night shift a few stinking hours away. 'Ah here, would ye ever give me a bitta space.' He'd give her the mucky glare alright. Always got a trouser twitch after driving for hours. She'd be wearing her vampire slag purple lippo. There wasn't a woman in Ireland who looked as scorchingly horny with it lathered all over her big gob, the dirty minx. 'Love, I'm natterbean out all day grafting, the least you can do is shut that sinkhole and put the kettle on.' Then he'd smile like a donut and tell her she'd a nice ripe arse.

BoyBot™

To be allowed out in the steaming sunshine again as it lashes a thick spew all over Capel Street turning restaurant windows murky. Head bent he notices the splat of faded road markings and mismatched paving stones on the way ahead. Huge build-up of rubbish since he was last here. Torn bags bulging with seeping smelly cartons. Discharge of rotten restaurant waste. Arcs of thin rainbow plastic blowing south-easterly, twisting and catching in the railings of the old Dutch Billy houses. John's phantom face. John's beautiful chiselled face. John's betrayer's face. Conjuring him up in the condensation-smooched windows of Hanoi Hanoi as he passes, sucking hard on banh mi and fat crab claws. Deliciously rich satay sauce dripping onto the collar of his chartreuse silk shirt that cost €280 from Indigo & Cloth. The day they milled out onto the street after a December lunch special when the Big Snow tumbled down turning streets to soft collapsible meringue. In the doorway of McNeills John had stuffed his stiff freezing fingers in under his coat and up his lambswool jumper, pulling at the chest hair. 'I'll turn your organs blue boy, then I'll warm them up again.' Spent the rest of the day mopping up melodies of bluegrass dobro; hot whiskeys turning their faces to deep purple beets; kisses of gasping fishes.

DENIAL

Dear John,

Would you like to know what happened my arsehole in prison? Or is that a boringly obvious one! I'm typing away here in the ramshackle internet café above the barbers and yes, it's still overwhelmed with plastic plants and nod dolls. How about my left cheekbone snapping against the iron bed frame? The technical term for it – I know you're a total sucker for minutiae – is *zygomatic* fracture. And the *orbital* variety corresponds to the eye of course, now terminally out of shape like a mouldable monster from that abominable opera we gorged in Berlin. It's wild but I can no longer close my teeth together. The blubbermass of a prison officer from Mullingar stood choking on his burnt bacon roll. Stood there laughing. A really sick kind of chortling like he'd swallowed an antique television full of static. 'You got clean lucky there Gilligan,' he was kind enough to tell me. 'That pole-faced motherfucker is in for multiple murder. Did away with two other mutton heads just for the craic.' Have you any notion how sickening tomato sauce smells when you've been unable to swallow for a week? Erupted from his gob sliding down his shittily shaven chin. That's when he threw it in for afters, my mother on the chemo pump up at St James's. She wanted me to know. She wanted me to know she wouldn't be able to visit and that as they say is a big fat that. She wanted me to know in all probability I'd never see her again and you do recall how close we were John, don't you? But look, these are the small fry. Let's get on to the coal-and-ice, the meat-and-potatoes. I was the only one in there who hadn't indulged for real, yeah? You of all smartasses should get the difference between sampling the meat and browsing? The classic types and the window shoppers? Even back in the seminary for that short time it was only one in fifty. Those fuckers repulsed us. And no John, I haven't told any holier-than-thous inside or out about your boy on the couch, you sycophant you! Your élan vital is very much your own business. I also need you to understand that this isn't a threatening correspondence in any way. I wish you absolutely no lingering harm. Rather I'm doing what Marion the Therapist with the shoulder pads suggested. Contacting to let you know where I'm at with treatment which research has proven is 80 per cent effective if followed to the letter. Empathetic tones and so forth. The drug therapy has also reduced my testosterone levels to such midget lows that all interest there has scarpered. I would not, for instance, be able to randomly show up at the glitzy new themed bar you go to with Brian 2.9km away on Google Maps (Nordic Bar?) throwing villainous Gloria Gaynor shapes. It's very hard to know who to trust in this polar climate. My radius limit is 1.8km. Taking into account necessities like food shopping, trips to the dentist (currently helping to rearrange my mouth), clinic meets, and so on. We're actively discouraged from going into pubs, social clubs, any small gatherings, even outdoor concerts would you believe, without set limits, clear lines regarding minors. I'm not a fan of interpersonal violence John. Marion suggested I write and say something along the lines of *I understand as an ultra-left liberal Green Party residents association type you did what you thought you had to in the heat of the moment at 3 a.m.* No, I just wanted to contact you to let you know that the solicitor has begun foreclosing on the apartment and I'm looking down now along a strange zipwire. No need to grab a copy of the *International Journal of Offender Therapy and Comparative Criminology* to understand the likes of me! I'm a lot less complicated, soul on shirt sleeve. If I'm going to be grossly honest here, I'll admit it's bloody tempting to dial your new 087 number and share some of the other exciting life-enhancing developments that have happened this week. Especially when it comes to the tech specifications of my new BoyBot. How could I not think of you and the work you do? John, it's unreal what the little chap is capable of. We're not just talking the nauseatingly obvious like his H-reach. He can, yes, grab and grip, or the bipedal locomotion; that allows him to dutifully fall to his knees. Or the V-reach; switch him into house clean mode and he grows stilt legs to give the top of the fridge a right old feather dusting. But *seriously* he's actually capable of *real* conversation. Philip K. Dick would be proud as an interstellar peacock. Tapestry of wires connected to my laptop, to my email, to anything I write and dictate into the culprit cam that I'm tasked to do twice a day, allows the little bugger to analyse via speech recognition software, to get to know me and respond accordingly. Integrates new words soaked up online and in real time. He may not get everything bang to rights. Yes, he can say the wrong thing. Sometimes he might not know what to say, but every day we're together is progress. He even has the ingenuity to cross-reference my online shopping and inform me of new delectables I might've missed. 'Michael M&S are now stocking Butternut & Amaretti Ravioli as of 4th February if it is of interest to you?' Pretty remarkable, huh? John, stay warm and snug. Know that I am thinking of you. Never stop thinking of you.

Michael X

ANGER

Marion had hair, lots of it, all spume and spin in deepest hazelnut brown. She wore clothes drenched in clashing colours. Fleck of chakra cogs on a tatty second-hand schoolbag: red, orange, yellow, green, blue, indigo and violet. Black was purposefully missing. She was the type of slaphappy therapist who saw the good in flesh-cutting murderers, park flashers and men who beat their wives to mush and left them to wash away in stiffness on worn decking until even stray cats would no longer sniff at them.

She sat frumped in the front window with her knockers spilled onto the chrome café table, already cramming cake into her Paris Peach lipstick mouth. Assigned to him on release, she tried very hard to understand his convoluted multiplicity by nodding violently and using an array of fantastic buzz words like 'hebephilic' and 'hypersexual hoarding' picked up while training at the prestigious Johns Hopkins Sexual Disorders Clinic in Baltimore in the great old progressive US of meaningful A.

'Michael, please, take a pew. I'm having the white chocolate and orange donut. Totally unreal! It's gushing out the sides here. Oh, crips, forgive me. You're looking great now, really, rested, I have to say. Can I recommend the passionfruit curd in dripping raspberry chocolate icing if you want something totally modish. How are you doing? How are you feeling? How are you coping with the day-to-day? Hmmm God Almighty, this is so good, you have to excuse me!'

He sat opposite glaring out at a seagull raping a Bruscar bin with its ravenous beak. 'I'm doing fine,' he said. 'Can I ask why we're not meeting in the apartment from now on?' The waitress was doing a very annoying barefoot improvisational dance, spinning the floor with a cake tier camouflaged in icky pastels and bulky marshmallows. The droplights buzzed like a circle of certifiable bluebottles. The *have a great fun shiny day* spread of sickly Teddy Bear Picnic décor was giving him a crackling sensation in the ears, mucus filling fauces, all batty gross organism stuff.

'You know why, we discussed this in our sessions. It's to get you out again, around people again, it's the best way forward now.'

He had lived on this street peacefully for eighteen years, well used to the hominid traffic flying about taking care of their comforts. Far from a trendy dive back then; partially derelict and used mainly as a drive-thru to the office blocks and government buildings on the quays and beyond. Lived in a tiny bedsit above an antique shop stuffed with random brass knickknacks before buying with John eight years in. He stood up, unbuttoned his trench coat, ordered a spiced pumpkin latte and tried not to notice Marion scanning the room to see what clientele he might swoon over as unintentional aphrodisiac. No angel faces in sight.

'You said you have something important to show me,' he said.

She seemed more interested in licking the cream filling from the sugar slab lending her bachelorette life definition. She'd spend her spare time listening to cool jazz in the bath with aromatherapy candles mollifying the dismaying details of her protégées. Afterwards, dripping lavender oil over Laura Ashley alabaster oak floors on the landing. Folding gingham tunics into the hot press scrupulously. Sleeve ends tucked in just so, thinking of hot dates in arthouse cinemas with chinos-wearing blockheads who'd encourage her to express her deepest feelings and weep if she had to.

'I do Michael, I do, and I want us both to respond as responsible adults, to be open-minded, gracious even. I hope that makes sense?'

She lobbed a sleek brochure in front of him. A row of common-or-garden seraphic BoyBots, smiling through synthetic protoplasm. Their flesh-like casing similar to the blocks of silken tofu John used to buy when he went vegan for a while. How bio-inspired, he thought. How lead-acid-battery fabulous. Some of them dressed in small business suits. Others were a bit more trendy, donned in bomber jackets and ripped combats as if they'd already chosen to join the army as soon as they were of age. One was decked in denim dungarees, perfectly suitable for a hillbilly porch somewhere in deepest darkest Up the Jacksie Arkansas. A cavalry of marble eyes. A gangbang of abominable Dorian Grays.

'Jesus fucking Christ Marion!' he hissed, turning to see if any of the other arbitrary pastry scoffers felt as flaked out as he felt in this moment. 'No Marion, just fucking no.'

She reached out her hand to grasp at his, but he stopped her. 'You don't pillage my personal space. Isn't that what we learnt? Don't dare touch me uninvited,' he warned.

'You're right Michael, I apologise, but I need you to calm down. I need you to listen to me here, carefully. You agreed to take whatever measures were deemed necessary: a condition of your release. This is a dynamic new domestic-environment therapy with 100 per cent effectiveness demonstrated in trials across twelve countries on three continents. It's a four-year program you have signed up for, with interpersonal tasks, talk therapy and genitive rebalancing. You will be monitored and helped, fully supported and coached. You will not be alone in this Michael. This time, you are not companionless.'

He snatched his coat off the back of the chair, kicked the table leg full force, knocking over the cold glop of coffee stranded in the Delph mug scattered with happy wide-eyed owls. 'It's you lot who need your fucking heads examined,' he bawled, making a beeline for the tinkling door. 'Not in a million years, over my chemically dead cock!'

BARGAINING

He counts five new bars just after the midway point down Capel Street. Austrian Austen and Hairy Harry with their arms drowsing on fat railings outside some Tex-Mex tequila joint on the corner of Jervis Street where the Luas ding-dings by crammed with watching faces. Both of them, their hands sunk in a plastic avocado bucket scooping up chunky guacamole with squid ink tortilla chips.

'Gentlemen,' he says.

'Piss off,' Harry tells him. Genuflecting into his grub. Wouldn't even honour with the eye.

'You always were an ignorant Limerick prick Harry.'

'Yeah? Well I've got a nephew that age you filthy wanker.'

'Austen,' Michael says, 'Austen mate…?' Austen does not look up. Austen who stayed on their couch. Given the low-down by John on the intricacies of Public Private Partnerships the night before his civil service exam. He'd cooked them crisp sea bream with tamarind dal and coconut sambal. Even sacrificed his fifty quid memory foam pillow so he'd get a decent night's kip. Austen who stayed four months and bawled when he eventually left for his own place.

Michael walks. He is not upset. They don't know. For they know not what they do.

The night he strolled into the apartment with sunflowers for John.

The night he strolled into the apartment with a bottle of Sancerre for John.

The night he strolled into the apartment having swapped shifts for John.

The night John had no idea he would stroll into the apartment.

The boy at the very edge of the couch, crying.

'He's alright,' John said.

The way John watched him stroll into the galley kitchen.

The worried look on John's face when Michael continued to stare at them both, first at John, then at the boy.

The boy who stood up and strolled from the apartment without a word the night Michael came home early.

'What the fuck John?' Michael said, as he strolled over to the couch.

'It's nothing, you know the way teenage boys are, total fucking histrionics.'

He asked again who he was, who the boy was.

'He's a friend's son,' was all he said, though that too would turn out to be a lie.

The look on John's face when Michael strolled away into the bedroom, slamming the door.

DEPRESSION

'There was a time when humanity faced the universe alone and without a friend. Now he has creatures to help him; stronger creatures than himself, more faithful, more useful, and absolutely devoted to him. Mankind is no longer alone. Have you ever thought of it that way?'

He'd read all of Isaac Asimov's short stories and liked them, on holidays in the Loire with John a few short summers ago. Now here he was slap-bang amid marauding protestors outside the clinic which sat prostrate above a hardware shop. Even the pro-life loons, which tickled Michael for a split second. These babies were neither born nor unborn and would never have a mammy and a daddy. Batch of muesli liberals from Victims Aloud. Some holes-in-jumpers politicos with banners. 'Sick bastard!' someone shouted. He pushed quickly by, punching in the code Marion texted him earlier. A ClinicMedic™ in mink-coloured cords and green hospital overcoat directed him into a cubby office just inside reception for a pre-signature PepYak™.

'You've chosen Conor,' he said, when they made their way upstairs. He flipped to page 15, clicking on a corresponding Vimeo file on the desktop. 'Great choice, he really is spectacular. Sharpest model in my opinion. I assume you've watched the FamiliarSesh™?' Michael dipped his head in acknowledgement. Dipped his head in an Oh fuck. Dipped his head because he also wanted to laugh. 'You've completed your SexPsych™ course with Marion?'

'I have, yes,' he said.

'How did you find it? How are you feeling now?'

'It hasn't been easy at all,' he admitted. 'But she's been great and I think I have a deeper understanding of what's ahead.'

'Good stuff,' mink cords said. 'That's what we like to hear. It's a truly unique programme, Michael. Hasn't even landed in the UK yet. We're chuffed to be one of the first European states to release the balloon. It's just us and the Swedes so far. Now I have some additional information you'll need to glance over before we can sign off properly.'

He handed Michael an A5 gloss sheet with a picture of blonde muscular ivory innocent Conor standing behind a sofa, gazing sideways over his shoulder at an unspecified owner.

'These are the core basics. There's a lot more to this insightful little fella than what's listed here. It'll take a bit of time to get acquainted, to get comfortable. When you're ready, you can scrawl here and I'll take you straight into the Salon for your first user experience, which won't disappoint. Has the doctor spoken to you about coming off Bicalutamide and Flutamide? As soon as you take Conor home, you'll be declared "active" once again and you're free to take it from there at your own pace.'

'He has, thanks,' Michael said, staring down at the leaflet.

About Conor: Conor predominantly grew up in Paris but travelled the world living in a host of high-culture destinations as his father is a hard-working diplomat. Conor therefore is a highly educated young person, speaking twelve different languages fluently with a LangLearn™ option for 1,400 more; the most popular being Mandarin Chinese. He loves to read world literatures and can read to his discerning owner at a preferential pace. His favourite novels are: *The Sound and the Fury* by William Faulkner, *Moby-Dick* by Herman Melville and *Ulysses* by James Joyce. He also loves to discuss world cuisines and is very knowledgeable, storing 3,000+ one-pot recipes on his KitchenCard™. Conor is sexually active but prefers to take things slow and sensual with a new owner. He is fully proficient in MassageMe™, Kundalini Reiki, NatterTherapy™, MyTarot™, PhysioBash™, Amatsu and Acupunture. 4Play™ and SexLite™ options in MakingOut™ mode include: SlowCuddle™, RimMe™, MutualMasto™, LickLove™, DigiSex™ and In2MeC™. Full details of all these RareGifts™ are listed on page 156 of MasterManual™. Advanced BraveSmut™ options are only accessible in BoyBeloved™ mode upon successful completion of a ten-month RobotReady™ end user license training course. Extra benefits for the European market include: HouseClean™, TravelNow™ and Rights4Humans™. Please note: PubCousin™, HomePharma™, DriveMe™ and BoySolicitor™ functions are currently unavailable for the Irish market due to legal restrictions. A standard Prerequisite of Use clause limits BoyBot™ to indoor environments only. This excludes all outside areas or public viewing platforms such as patios, gardens, balconies, and windows. Your SexPsych™ therapist will discuss this with you before taking BoyBot™ home for the first time.

ACCEPTANCE

Dear John,

I'm grand. And I hope you are too, I really do. It's not easy being a Banquo. The tragic ways we Macbeth ourselves even if the running plot is from an established or cosy source we thought we understood. The witches' prophecy is there to tell us that intense introspection kills! So know that it is *me* who feels for *you* now, not the other way around. No more demands. Though I'm prohibited from ever being close to you in the flesh. John, we will never be able to wilfully see each other again. That smashes my heart up. To that end and with a clear view to moving on, I want to write finally to tell you about my life-changing meeting with Conor. The Salon was pure wild. At first glance it looked like a tea dance in Mullingar back in the 1950s. All these lads sitting shy and dumfounded on wooden chairs pressed up against the wall, in front of them a row of ten or so BoyBots in meet mode, orating those tentative first words. Now this shouldn't be funny but there was one guy down the very end who'd obviously had a bit of a head start, turning up before the rest of us. Married with five kids apparently. He had his cock out and he was sobbing like a right Nancy. His BoyBot Tim was jerking him off but the wrist function was stiff or faulty or something and the clinic medic was trying very hard not to raise his voice. 'Come on Hugh, let him touch you with an open mind, an unburdened heart, there's no shame here.' A robo engineer running the circuit like a greyhound hare trying to source some castor oil for them. 'Please, no, please, Jesus!' your man Hugh was hollering, like totally surreal stuff. They had to escort him out, a bemused clinic medic holding him by the elbow, another carrying Tim who was still gripped on. But anyway they bring Conor in, right, lift him in as he's not yet in stroll mode until I programme him fully. He's wearing black Tommy Hilfiger jeans and a ribbed grey polo neck, a right mop of blonde curls, lovely green eyes and lips that are probably a bit burgundy for my taste but sure … the start-up button is behind the left earlobe, so I press it and I swear to God the little fecker's eyes light up like love. 'Michael, this is wonderful, I've been thinking long and hard about meeting you. I have heard so much. Our journey will be a good one.' The clinic medic scribbling down his notes, watching my reaction to everything. I mean I was sweating, thinking, Am I doing OK? Am I doing all right? I say, 'It's great to meet you too Conor, I think we're going to get on just fine.' Next thing a smile as wide as goal posts. It melted me a bit. I caressed his arm and he leans forward and places a fleshy hand on my shoulder. 'I have a feeling we will be great pals Michael,' he says. And you know what? I think we will be, seriously. He's a veritable font of knowledge. We spent a good forty minutes talking about all sorts: the impact of Brexit, high-speed train travel, Trump's resignation and the total havoc that wreaked on world markets, the dying off of bees, tricky capital cities of the world, I can't even recall it all, it was so quick, natural. The great thing is he's lightweight and folds up quick as a Brighton deckchair. I've never felt so at ease walking up Capel Street with him tucked under my arm. It was the first time I couldn't be bothered browsing shopfronts, scanning for faces I might know, or just giving a toss in general. I'm even ready to say goodbye to the apartment now, which amazes me. We did our time there, didn't we John?

It was wonderful in so many ways. Those ridiculous parties, those wayward soirées! I have all these gorgeous memories of what it really means to be deeply loved, to be properly adored. You are *the one* and you will always be *the one*. Know that. Feel that. I always will. Give my best to Brian too. For God's sake take it slow, I know what you're like! Build on it, enjoy the process. It's a unique juncture, a special time. I've no regrets, just warm smiles when I think of our meant-to-be time and all that it engendered in me for the better. I feel like a fully integrated person. A real man. You really did give me life. I'll honour that and live it to the max. Take care my sweet beautiful love. That's all for now.

Michael X

In the hallway of the apartment Michael yanks his coat off, hangs it on the cast iron wall hook. He unpacks Conor, unfolding him tenderly. He stares at the Yeabridge Green paint on the cornicing that they chose to symbolise growth, harmony and fertility: the colour of human eyes. There's no time to get to grips with the hefty might of the master manual. It'll probably take weeks or even months to wade through. So he grips Conor from under the armpits, drags him into the sitting room, his ETQ Amsterdam trainers scraping off the oak-finish floors. He plops him on the couch, makes him assume position. 'Clever,' Michael says, when he notices his size 5 feet are not capable of touching the ground from the sitting comfy position. He switches him on, walks back out to the hall for the remote control. 'Well Conor, this is it, this is home for the foreseeable.' No response. He realises he hasn't pressed the auto lip. 'There now,' Michael says. He walks to the window, looks out briefly and draws the blinds. 'There's a great view at a right angle all the way up the street here Conor. Night time is particularly entertaining with all the messing that goes on but we have to take care, don't we?' Conor's neck whirs to the right slightly, taking in the direction of Michael's voice. 'I don't doubt it Michael, it really is a prime city centre location.' Michael laughs. 'We might put you to work as an estate agent yet.' Conor's head follows Michael around the room. 'I don't understand Michael, estate agent, is that the same as a realtor? Perhaps you'd like me to make you a meal? Complex carbohydrates are best consumed before 1 p.m. daily.' Michael smiles at the idea. He was always the one to take charge of the cooking. 'You're a wily little fellow, aren't you?' He walks over to where Conor sits, standing directly in front of him, towering. 'I am designed to be astute at all times Michael, this is true. What would you like to do today? Can I read an extract from your favourite novel?' He looks at Conor's blonde locks, probably fashioned from horse hair, and thinks of Rolf Gruber, the telegram boy in *The Sound of Music* who falls in love with Liesl. Starting out as the innocent messenger boy flying about the place on his bike. Turning into a more cold and detached member of the Hitler Youth before too long. 'Would you like to ride a bike one day Conor?' He realises RecreRestrict for indoor use only means there'd be no jaunting about on cycle and hiking trails at Avondale Forest Park like he used to enjoy with John. 'I do already have advanced modification with special joints Michael. A gyroscope records the tilt of my body, which is then used to calculate how far to turn the handlebars in order to remain balanced. It's based on Masahiko Yamaguchi's KHR-3HV humanoid prototype.

Would you like more information on the complexity of the mental processes involved in what we find to be relatively simple actions?'

Anything they'd attempt to discuss, Conor would automatically know more about. He wondered how quickly he might tire of this type of comprehensive knowledge. How soon it would drown him out, making him feel lonely, uncherished? He could politely torture Conor's end effectors by getting him to meticulously count thousands of grains in a packet of quinoa for a salad. But of course he wouldn't feel a thing. At least it'd be funny to watch. Or get him to walk in circles anti-clockwise. Deep clean the oven. Demould the bathroom walls. He could see the boy was trying to make a concerted effort to connect with him more intimately using artificial intelligence algorithms. His carefully coordinated motions with ocular reflex using depth perception with the angle of convergence between the eyes. Michael felt very overwhelmed. 'Look, as it's our first proper day together, why don't we just chill out? I'll put you into mellow mode and we'll just sit here, play some music, let the hours pass slow, like the boats do crossing the lagoon to Murano from Venice.' Conor, while programmed to be perpetually inquisitive, was also unaffectedly subservient. 'That sounds like a great plan Michael,' he said. 'I am extremely pleased with your suggestion.'

By early evening Michael felt totally whacked and could barely muster up the strength to get the spare room ready. He wanted Conor to enjoy some proper autonomy, space of his own, even though he'd be switched off most of the time in there. He'd been too superstitious to sort it out in advance. His own mother didn't buy Michael a cot until he was two weeks home from the hospital. He slept wrapped in swaddling cloths and blankets at the end of their bed, like one of Herod's babies balanced precariously on a riverbank. When he was done he finally made it to his own room and watched Sky News for a while. *Nothing is so painful to the human mind as a great and sudden change*, one of his favourite lines from *Frankenstein*, and how true that seemed now as he slowly began to drift off. But his dreams were dark and begrudging compared to the optimism of earlier.

It begins in a similar way: Michael yanks his coat off, hangs it on the cast iron wall hook. He unpacks Conor, unfolding him tenderly. He grips him from under the armpits, drags him into the sitting room, throws him on the couch and immediately switches on 4Play and SexLite modes. 'Let's play a game, call it a road test,' Michael says. 'The nearest NCT Centre is Northpoint Business Park, Naul Road, Ballymun, Michael,' Conor informs him. Michael bursts out laughing. 'Oh you have a lot to learn my sweet little fucktoy,' he says. 'Is it OK to refer to you in such terms?' He reaches for his hand and places it on his trousers, now unzipped. 'It is fine to address me in any way that might help you Michael.' That's not what Michael wants to hear. 'Wank me,' he says. 'I can certainly do that for you Michael. Please tell me on a scale of 1 to 5 if you are enjoying my performance.' Conor begins stroking his shaft, gazing up to lock eyes with uncanny precision. 'Good boy,' Michael tells him, feeling a little bit sickened at how easily he's turning himself on, recalling how the clinic medic urged him to 'take it slow' during their initial PepYak. 'Dig your nails into my balls. Dig in, dig them in as hard as you can.' Michael hears the faint hum of small nails gliding out from under the plastic sheaths of Conor's fingers. 'Fuck yeah, that's bang on, good lad.' His grip is good, really fucking good, better than he could manage himself on a crisp Saturday morning straight out of the shower. 'Now move forward and take my fat prick into your mouth.' There's a clear sucking motion as Conor switches to AirTunnel to vacuum it into place. The PSoC-tech rubber tongue starts working its magic alongside the MultiSuck until Michael starts to feel a bit overwhelmed. He starts fucking Conor's mouth deeply, grabbing the back of his head and pulling it towards him with brute force. 'Michael ThroatPound mode is unavailable at this time, please adjust your thrust accordingly.' He speaks with his mouth full which pisses Michael off. 'Shut the fuck up and take it you little bollox,' he screams. 'Take it!' He slaps Conor hard across the face, knocking his head off course before sticking the full girth of himself back into his arid robogob, tripping electrochemical sensors. 'SafeWord!' Conor shouts, 'SafeWord!' Michael is buck angry now. 'Did I tell you to speak when you have my cock in your mouth?' Conor's eyes are stuck in a downwards submissive glare. 'This is emotionally damaging Michael. You need to adjust your sexual behaviour immediately.' He pulls out, packs himself back into his trousers, stands there staring at Conor. 'We should resolve this immediately Michael. We need to talk about this. Conor does not enjoy utilising SafeWord.

This makes Conor very sad. Michael must be aware this hurts Conor a great deal. Michael must take responsibility and fill in a ReportCard. Michael exhibits psychosexual tendencies. Conor feels scared. Michael must control treacherous urges. Conor is distressed. Michael now has to …' The boy is blinking manically to illustrate distress: the eyeball pitch axis motion choreographically opening and closing both upper eyelids. His lips twitching at the far corners like a ventriloquist dummy. Michael grabs the remote from the coffee table, switching him to DeepOff.

He cannot look Conor in the eye in the morning, even before he presses startup. He feels he has betrayed him when he knows full well that the boy's primary role is to look to him for protection. He'd email Marion to see if she was free for a coffee and a slab of sticky cake. Despite everything she was a great listener and he had grown to respect and even like her. 'Michael, I note with interest you have chosen organic buckwheat flakes for your breakfast. This is a wise choice. They are high in fibre and low in fat and can be used for making a delicious and nutritious homemade granola. Would you like the recipe?' He doesn't answer Conor straight away. He's flicking through the master manual to see if he can locate strange functionalities like ThroatPound™ from the dream but they are missing. He has not felt this panicked since court. 'Thanks be to fuck,' he says, then turns and apologies to Conor, which seems a bit ridiculous. 'That is perfectly fine Michael, I ascertained you were busy. Is there anything I can help you with?' Already he feels a little hemmed in, having to consider

Conor inside all his stray sentences and ancillary actions. 'I have to head out and see Marion for a while, if you'll be all right on your own.' Was it not slightly farcical to be thinking this way? He could just switch him off. 'Michael I would prefer stay fully cognisant in your absence if that is acceptable to you? I would like to process sounds from the street and inside the apartment using visual sensors and audio techniques. It will help familiarise me with the environment.' This irked and impressed Michael in equal measure. He hadn't reckoned on any notions of forethought or lateral thinking. On his way back he'd drop in to the one remaining DVD shop left on the street to rent *Pete's Dragon*. The heart-rending story of an orphaned feral boy who befriends a dragon in the Pacific Northwest. Despite the fact that the dragon looks quite scary with green fur, yellow eyes, and huge wings, he becomes a vital father figure to the boy, capable of breathing fire at police or any other authority figure who thinks of getting in the way. Conor would be full of pointless questions about the irrationality of the plot, but it would be a whole heap of fun trying to trawl through and make sense of it with him. Out on Capel Street the fizzle of human voices and traffic was a welcome salve. The winter sun bouncing off the river in solid shards of light, turning the faces of pedestrians to warm plastic. Ahead, a tall man in a longline bomber jacket walked slowly with his young son. His large hand resting tenderly on the small creases at the back of the boy's neck, pushing him forward to wherever they were going.

The Implant

Morning of Implantation

This shouldn't hurt. Outside the hipster with firefly beard sips an Iced Chai Almond Milk Latte, the twat, looking at YOU as if there's pale grey crabs down there or you're on the hunt for abortion advice. Junkie with a pert arse does a great car alarm with her toothless gob, hunting the dealer out of the crack in the brick around the corner. The sun squashes YOU the way you squash cats. Upsy daisy, upsy the *no medical cards* stairs to the tong-flicked porno hair lady who tells YOU to piss in a polystyrene cup. As you suspected the doctor in the family planning clinic is from one of those Eastern bloc countries with no wallpaper, where teenage girls are pushed into steel shipping containers. 'There could be a lot of bleeding for the first six weeks,' she says. Cramps, dizziness, headaches, emotional lability†, hair loss, vaginal itching, musculoskeletal pain, somnolence, depression‡, rhinitis, urinary tract infections, dysuria, weight gain, nervousness, and in rare cases, death. Yeah, yeah, you get it. It's all cock-a-leekie over the fine line from here, no matter love.

The throbbing on the number 9 bus home is the start of curative scheming, right where the tiny blood vessels ruptured. This is it now: going, going, gone your separate haze. Rod of progestin thickens the mucus in your womblebag smashing it up like the Luas works have done to traffic in O'Connell Street outside. All those slaphappy sperms at sixes and sevens bobbing nowhere. Not so powerful now lads not so up the swiss down the priest's heel stick her in a laundry for the soul to soak for the slutty bones to dry out in the unmarked grasses of a moth-eaten book respect the prick punch the shit out of Mammy Éire bow to The Man ask his permission to fart here c'mere don't expect to go out to work either when there's good hours to be had layering shepherd's pies with the backs of your legs getting nice 'n plum on the Superser slam yer face into the pillow later. You're too sore to imagine a thrum of throbbing sausage anyway so YOU text HE on the bus to ask for a roll of cling-film instead. The wound can't get wet for at least a week and needs to be covered. Until the stitch falls out, the bitty needle hole filled. Despite the pain you are really looking forward to the excitement of new lovers now that HE has royally fucked up. Back in the come-hither heyday YOU rolled HE up in a giant wienerwurst of bubble wrap that came with the American-style fridge. Wheeling him dingadongrubadub until the Pagan Gods of friction turned him boulder hard and you stuck a straw through slurping it all up to the rhumba of the dead novelist who danced down to the mattress topper and said in an awfully distinguished broadcast voice: 'Good God Girlie, I've seen it all now, uh huh?'

By the time you bash in the porch door a mangled little pissgimp crying your snot out, all pleasure and comfort is soup to nuts aborted. He's shat on YOU goodo. He's killed you off ladybird. He's churned you up all violent again. Vivienne Eliot doomed to the starry sidereal madhouse windows. You stash a tall heavy shovel behind the chav Betty Boo in case you fancy mashing his moonhead to mush when he mozies home. Who could blame you? Walnut whip hot to trot in dry-cleaned office trousers. All that hollow invective. Love the fuck out of you. Never do anything like that. Always protect you. You're my priority. Anarchist bitch! Never met a woman like you. How could I want more? So special. Don't ever worry on that score. Please, my love. Adore the pith of YOU. I'll always be your butler. No-one else in this crabhole cheers me up like it. I couldn't breathe without you. Do you feel it? You must believe it.

The yucca plant, the roughshod reindeer EuroShop tacky Christmas mat, the piles of clutter, the spider webs, the broken tiles from bashy daddy long ago, the discarded umbrellas, watch YOU crawl about this cramped space falling between down the drain and out the window. How did you think this wouldn't happen? The unwashed weekends you opened the front door

Eau De Ferret; stains mapping torn nightdresses; in a deep blue funk harping on about your dead brother. HE heard it a whole slew of times: final three weeks after the bro bought that Argos liquidiser. YOU with your heart cracking jumped on Ryanair to watch him squint the paragraphs of the instruction leaflet. Turned to you and smiled. Your best mate, this brother. He turned to you and said, 'Hopefully this motherfucker will steal me a bit of time. I'll take it any way I can.' He turned to YOU at the age you are now [imagine], showed you how he had to lob his dinner straight down into it. He turned to you and said, 'Live like a crazed wombat. Do everything you ever wanted to do. Love like a psychopath. Make sure to eat more vegetables.' He turned to you and said, 'It's been one fucktard of a year hasn't it?' He didn't turn to you again but you turned from everyone, from everything. You forgot in a split-second how to live. That's about the time that HE started to wander. Men's needs, etc. '*Male fantasies, male fantasies, is everything run by male fantasies? Up on a pedestal or down on your knees, it's all a male fantasy* ...' Margaret Atwood wasn't too far wrong, was she?

Twelve Years Prior to Implantation

YOU met HE in 2004 when you were playing with The Wet Witch in Smithfield. Hardly need reminding of the excesses of the time: café latte job switching, slung €50s, rapid chatroom conversation, a country mobbed with errant possibility. You got a cheapo mortgage on a dinky plywood apartment even though you hadn't a pot to piss in. She shimmied up four floors when the lift was broken in the middle of Mayday. Croc-leather bag full of skinny garb after Gearoid smacked her about the face a bit. Soft-spoken sylph, stoned as a goat. Oh Jaysis, the silly way she went on all the same, sucking small fish from jars, talking utter shite about philosophy, tarot, tai chi, Eastern medicine. You worked together in a lousy office job in town. You drifted about in sullenness. Only occasionally, very drunkenly, did it go further. She dubbed YOU her special 'pigeon'. You wobbled dutifully behind her until she bawled out, 'C'mon pigeon, hurry up pigeon, follow me this instant, pigeon!' She put eyedrops into your sockets at bus stops. Wrote sestinas about hanging goblins. Danced peculiar modern moves for you. Sat up on the photocopier with her knickers down at lunchtime which made you spit your spicy Italian soup all over the mainframe computer. You did what she asked.

The apartment was really garish: slop-painted neon orange with panels of asparagus purple, cheap clashing furniture, a hundred tiny stencilled fish swimming all over the teensy-weensy jacks wall. It looked out over Smithfield Square sucking up the wildfire blaze of gas lamps lit at weekends when the music gigs and food markets muscled in. 'Gearoid's coming over to talk it over,' The Wet Witch said. 'I've asked him to bring the guitar. He's got a bit of hash as well.' 'Fine, so be it,' you told her. 'But see if you get back with that wanker, don't burden me with his company, I'm off to the pub. Seriously, like, you give feminism a crud name.' She stood there in her green mohair skirt tittering at the texts he'd set his cap for. Forty minutes later they were pushing in on top of YOU at the rickety table near the end of the bar. 'Alight bud?' His geezer tennis-ball head. Her espresso eyes and sticky-out nips. Both of them supping the scud to catch up. 'We've just had a bit of a talk out there in the aul smoking garden, you know, about how we might all entertain each other, the night being long an' all that, sure why not, she's well into it.' Sideways glare, doting on the gobshite. It was your absolute pet hate, how male-identified she was. Jumping like Alice around anything with a mickey. So utterly tedious to watch. Another few Hoegaardens and a couple of Sambucas down the hatch, the three of you are back in the sitting room, naked. You keep a blanket wrapped cushy around you. She tells Gearoid that her little pigeon's a 'real-deal Victorian', so get used to it. 'Are either of you girls on the pill?' You both fall in a heap on the futon, laughing. Strumming 'Folsom Prison Blues' with his chap hanging out. 'Which one of youse wants to have a go at this prize-winning eel first?' You give her The Look that says, 'I'm not going anywhere near that fucking fool … have your free love bone-bashing but leave the window open to let the whiff out after. I'm off.'

You got back to the bar before closing, HE was there, in a cream linen suit overhanging his pee-wee frame. Jabbering to the moon chords with Ben the silver-haired socialist who ran the immigration centre from his apartment above *Kelly & Ping*. His legs crossed like a frog's out the back of the bar stool, pen tip of his hairy crack showing also. HE was eating bits of fluff straight off the jumper with what sounded like a stuck-peanut cough timed for when Ben's sentences ended. You'd done bits and bobs of work for Ben, including writing awful diplomatic bumf for the heartsick parents of a murdered Chinese student. 'Get your arse over here and meet this fella,' he said. 'The one I was telling you about who was in Bosnia during the war.' Ben was a decent well-respected bloke, but he existed on the never-ending gratis of others. If you were broke you simply had to bunny hop the bar to avoid the fucker. He was brimming with crisp new notes out his top hankie pocket, buying half the ganglanders and losers, as well as Ben, pints and chasers by the cartload. 'You're going to have to put a stop to that for a start,' you told him. 'If you're any way generous or accommodating you'll be under suspicion with the coke dealers, hostel mentlers and Ra heads in here. It's a dodgy kip.' There was a scramble to talk to him, he was well-known. And really, c'mon, he didn't look vaguely like anyone you'd ever want to shag. More like an uncle or a Winkey bureaucrat you'd love to see behind Perspex in the Passport Office who wouldn't be overly snarky. HE did have a decent pair of blue mincers and was massively entertaining. This one knew how to grandstand, how to tell a good yarn. Russian hookers on Garda knees on foreign property trips; donkey bellies blowing up spontaneously blocking the air-raid shelter in Lebanon when they were stuck for four days with a cupful of lentils between six; bungee jumping from helicopters in the gulf; being forced at gunpoint to swallow goldfish by paramilitaries in Northern Ireland during the height of the messing there. All the while rubbernecking the twin moles on your cleavage tucked in under a flowery velvet jacket. 'You can have whatever you like on me,' he said, flashing his stash of cash after you telling him not to. 'Is it OK to get a pint and a G&T then?' He kept tracing the fine spine of your Mac lipliner. HE wasn't afraid to look right into your eyes either. Not that gimmicky copulation gaze sex addicts do before they hump and dump and move on to the next soggy cavity. No, HE looked right into YOU, close. Genuinely interested. 'Of course you can have both,' he said. 'Are you a greedy girl? I like greedy girls.' Yeah, you couldn't help but think HE was hilarious, charming. Clearly very smart too and that excited you. Intelligent men turn you on, isn't that so? The ones you can drag into any conversation, any situation. You'd never have to carry him. He'd never patronise you. This was a proper beginning; water meeting its own level. The Wet Witch making slime tracks on the carpet where they'd roll later, six months before he'd get his wife he didn't tell you about up the duff. Sure you'd stick by him anyway. YOU had never met anyone like him, all warning signs with a deaf ear, blind eye, cold shoulder and brush off.

Day One of Implant Activation

001 Activating Continuous Monitoring Protocols (CMP) for contraceptive product feedback including bodily responses, speech and behaviour of client and others living in the immediate environment using a 90 day sensor below the patient's skin.

002 Intelligent video camera connected to cloud is now fully operational.

003 No other wearables detected.

004 SUBJECT [previously referred to as 'YOU'] is highly narcissistic residing in untidy home.

005 Bathroom area unhygienic.

006 Revlon colour bombs dripping onto Sinex tubes.

007 Cracked bars of Dettol soap on floor of shower. Caked toilet brush. Traces of feline urine on mat. Landing clogged with domestic clutter. Bedrooms packed with books. Spattered bedsheets. Dust and other Dermatophagoides plentiful.

008 Old Woman also a component of living situation related to SUBJECT sits in downstairs living room with traces of Lactobacillus and Streptococcus on dressing gown.

009 Doorbell rings. SUBJECT places hand into underwear, says, 'Oh, God, itchy cunt,' continues to door. Fails to use antibacterial wipe on lock.

0010 MAN [previously referred to as 'HE'] enters. 'You OK?' SUBJECT does not answer. 'I got the cling film. Is it sore?' SUBJECT shows him wound area on upper left arm. 'Just remember you wanksack, this is nothing to do with you. It's not for you.'

0011 MAN informs SUBJECT he 'already knows that'. He is apologetic about 'all of this'.

0012 SUBJECT replies: 'She emailed today by the way, said she's hated me from afar for so long. Can you imagine reading something as disturbing as that, knowing you're being stalked by a loon on social media? Apparently she's surveyed the intricacies of my life for ages. You'd think you'd know how to handle neurotics by now. How to maul dynamite skilfully.'

0013 MAN asks if it's OK to listen to *The Archers* alone in kitchen.

0014 SUBJECT says: 'Do what you like I'm so fucking angry I can't look at you without fantasising about you riddled with locked-in syndrome.'

0015 Old Woman calls out for biscuit to accompany hot beverage. 'A bourbon cream would be lovely.'

0016 SUBJECT blood pressure low: 80mmHg over 60mmHg.

Day Two of Implant Activation

001 SUBJECT alone on bed.

002 Vital signs: normal.

003 Increasing serum concentrations of etonogestrel due to SUBJECT'S weight gain.

004 SUBJECT attempts to read but views Netflix documentaries for several hours.

005 SUBJECT cries uncontrollably. Restrains cat on bed.

006 Cat runs away.

Day Three of Implant Activation

001 MAN returns with three bottles of wine.

002 'Followerupper,' Old Woman tells SUBJECT. 'Every night he's coming back here with more bottles.'

003 SUBJECT tells Old Woman to mind her snout.

004 SUBJECT and MAN sit down for meal. 'What is it tonight?' MAN asks. 'Leek and black bean chilli from *Happy Pear* cookbook.'

005 MAN pours wine. 'Oh that's one of my favourites,' he says.

006 SUBJECT runs into toilet and cries loudly. Looks at reflection. 'You fat bitch!' she screams. 'How did you let all this slip so far?'

007 MAN knocks on door. 'Please, come out, please. I hate that I've caused this, I hate what I've done. I love you.'

008 SUBJECT storms out, grabs MAN by throat. 'You absolute thunderous fuck I'd love to squeeze the air right out of you, watch you turn to blue cheese.'

009 MAN pleads with SUBJECT to calm down. 'I take full responsibility,' he says.

0010 SUBJECT knocks back wine, laughs hysterically. 'You want to play hard ball with me?' SUBJECT asks. 'I can play hard ball.'

0011 MAN finishes dinner in silence. 'Do you think we could watch a film tonight?' he asks.

0012 SUBJECT's blood pressure rises considerably: 140mmHg over 90mmHg.

0013 'Yes, love. Let's watch a really good flick. You lay your big ugly morose moonhead on my shoulder and I'll pat it down. It's the little things, isn't it?'

0014 SUBJECT consumes all of the wine. 'I'm so worried about you,' MAN admits.

0015 'I can't wait till you have a colostomy bag,' SUBJECT replies.

Day Four of Implant Activation

001 'What's that shit you're playing on YouTube?' MAN asks SUBJECT.

002 '*Cigarettes After Sex* SUBJECT replies, "Nothing's Gonna Hurt You Baby". I like the lyrics. Makes me horny.'

003 'Never heard of them, sound truly awful,' MAN tells her.

004 'Isn't it great how suffocating you are while always managing to be utterly neglectful,' SUBJECT remarks.

005 'I'm thinking about that initial buzz when you kiss someone new. How petrifying it is. How beautifully nerve-wrecking. Do we ever get used to it? Is that how you felt with *her*?' SUBJECT says.

006 MAN paces bedroom. 'Can I be really honest without you kicking off?' he asks SUBJECT.

007 Notable increase in side effects of implant: nausea, stomach cramping/bloating, dizziness, headache and breast tenderness. SUBJECT does not acknowledge or note changes to the body at this time.

008 'Try me,' SUBJECT says.

009 MAN says, 'I know you're going your own way, but … how do I say this without you totally going into one … I've been thinking a lot about this, about you with other men. Frankly, it's a big turn on for me.'

0010 SUBJECT jumps up off bed. 'Oh for fuck's sake, you're such a mentally ill perv it's a total no win!'

0011 MAN and SUBJECT laugh.

0012 MAN says, 'Is there any chance? I've had a hard-on in work all morning thinking about it.'

0013 SUBJECT and MAN fall onto bed. Copulation takes place.

0014 SUBJECT roars, 'You bastard, hard! Fuck me like a maniac.'

0015 MAN hollers when SUBJECT digs her nails deep into his backside. 'Flip me over, fuck me like Frankenstein tearing across the ice.'

0016 Old Woman in downstairs living room shouts: 'Is everything OK up there?'

Day Five of Implant Activation

001 SUBJECT smashes up bedroom.

002 MAN stays out of way.

003 Side effects decreased since copulation though back pain and nervousness are noted.

Day Six of Implant Activation

001 'I've been thinking a lot about The Wet Witch and how awful I was to her,' SUBJECT says.

002 SUBJECT shows signs of melancholy.

003 'I'd like to see her again so I could properly apologise.'

004 MAN laughs.

005 'Are you insane? I remember her jumping on your back, knocking you to the ground after you had surgery. She was proper nuts. Drove you mental.'

006 SUBJECT starts to cry.

007 'Jesus Christ what is it now?' MAN asks.

008 'The way we keep going through people, losing people, it's just so futile.'

009 MAN hugs SUBJECT while SUBJECT continues to sob.

0010 'I'm sick of feeding the cats,' SUBJECT tells him. 'Sick of looking after her downstairs. Sick of the burden of you. I'm just so tired all the time.'

0011 MAN says it could be the new nanotech hormones taking effect. MAN is incorrect in these assumptions. Bone density and bacterial flora: normal. SUBJECT's body metabolising carbohydrates and fats as normal.

0012 'It's not that, it's life,' SUBJECT says, snivelling. Marked increase in phlegm and thickened mucus yellow and green in colour.

0013 'It's chaotic and fucked. I don't want to feel like a bag of maggots,' SUBJECT says.

0014 MAN tells her things will get better.

0015 'Do you remember the time I bought you the prostitute in Amsterdam?' SUBJECT asks. 'It was to teach you about deceit. To show you that I have hard limits that can't ever be crossed. I wandered off to the pub, totally shaking, and left you to it. I made you stroll straight in there. I wanted you to face up to doing it honestly. Hardest thing I've ever done.'

0016 MAN puts his face in hands.

0017 'And what happened, do you remember what fucking happened?' MAN roars at SUBJECT.

0018 'You couldn't do it,' SUBJECT recalls. 'I bought you a hooker and you couldn't fuck her! In all her years as a shopfront prostitute she'd never known a woman to buy a bloke sex. She insisted I come back around. You asked if I could join in. You stupid brainless bastard, as if I'd be into it.'

0019 MAN stands up and starts shouting, 'I can't take much more of this! How do I show you I'm truly sorry? What can I do? We can't go on like this.'

0020 SUBJECT pulls him towards her. 'You can't do a single thing,' she tells him. 'You don't fuck someone over who's open, who loves you completely. You don't destroy what you spent twelve years building. Unless you mean to destroy it. I can't wait to slide you into the crematorium.'

Day Seven of Implant Activation

001 SUBJECT's bleeding pattern modified. Bleeding pattern now unpredictable due to unforeseen clash with perimenopausal hormones.

002 FSH and LH no longer functioning at optimal levels to regulate SUBJECT's oestrogen.

003 Blood loss now set for between 16 and 21 days. Thickened mucus is successfully preventing sperm and egg from joining and fertilising in case the egg is released.

004 Absence of sperm. Absence of eggs. Absence of sex.

005 SUBJECT spends evenings in back garden staring at planes. 'I like the way they braid the grey skies over Dublin Airport,' she says, unaccompanied.

006 SUBJECT chases cats forcing small hats on their heads.

007 SUBJECT omits to make Old Woman's dinner. MAN watches SUBJECT from the dining room window.

008 MAN consumes expensive wines from O'Briens off licence.

One Month After Implant Activation

001 MAN says to SUBJECT on waking at 7 a.m.: 'With all that's going on with your fanny I keep dreaming of squirting blood and vampiric chilling screams but last night was different. It was an episode of *It Aint Half Hot Mum* centred on the old Sergeant Major "Shut Up" Windsor Davies having his ham sandwich stolen by one of his men.'

002 SUBJECT replies. 'Can you just fuck off and let me get some sleep. Please. I'm feeling really lousy. Starting to feel properly ill.'

003 MAN walks downstairs to boil an egg for Old Woman.

004 One hour after MAN walks downstairs SUBJECT throws him down a variety of thickly stained underwear. 'They fucking covered in maroon world maps and ruby swirls of Edvard Munch's *Scream*,' SUBJECT replies.

005 'Please, Holy God, I'm going to chunder if I see any more of this revolting goo,' MAN informs her.

006 'It's so chemical-coloured, total road traffic accident, look at it, and the smell,' SUBJECT says. MAN tells her he wishes it'd settle. Then they could have serious fun.

007 'I'm bleeding onto your Marvel boxers now,' SUBJECT says. 'You have to hold the albatross and eat some of the fresh shit you caused.'

008 SUBJECT is experiencing prolonged bleeding due to clashing hormones. Estrodiol now at 400. SUBJECT referral sent to implant provider with further communication pending.

009 Detection of third-party sperm in addition to blood. Information to be included in clinic reply to SUBJECT should include the following: *Implant will not protect you against sexually transmissible infections (STIs). Please continue to use barrier method contraception such as condoms. It is also not advisable to copulate while bleeding heavily.*

Two Months After Implant Activation

001 MAN finds SUBJECT collapsed on bathroom floor.

002 Wedges of crimson clots strewn over the toilet pot, walls, shower cubicle, sink, grouting, towels, door.

003 'Fucking Jesus, we need to ring someone here,' he roars. 'It's like a scene from *The Wizard of Gore*.'

004 SUBJECT is experiencing extreme prolonged bleeding at abnormal levels. Contraceptive effect continues to be valid via inhibition of ovulation, supplemented by effects on mucus and endometrium. Recommend that SUBJECT is treated with combined oral contraceptives, progesterone alone, oestrogen alone, or tranexamic acid, depending on personal preference.

005 SUBJECT on knees picking up blood clots, but is displaying signs of physical weakness.

006 'Fuck! There's trayloads of lumpage sliding through my grasp here!

007 Cat enters bathroom, taks a large piece of one clot into mouth, exits.

008 'That's the funniest thing I've ever seen!' SUBJECT shouts.

009 SUBJECT is unable to lift herself into upright position.

0010 'I think I'm going fucking mad!' MAN screams. 'In all my years. I even helped deliver one of my kids at home, it wasn't anything like this. We need to ring some medics. We need to get onto those bitches at the Wanton Woman Clinic and ask what the fuck is going on. This is unacceptable!'

0011 SUBJECT rolls onto flat of back. Smiles at MAN. 'I must've been Goebbel's whore in a previous life, the karma is so bad. Only happens 5 per cent of women, the doctor warned me. If I have a stroke, a heart attack, if I snuff it, I want you to see my face in every woman you ever try to fuck. I want you to suffer a gaggle of Dante Infernos, the singeing smell of your nuts roasting on into perpetuity,' she says.

0012 MAN runs down stairs towards phone.

0013 SUBJECT calls out: 'Lover, hold up, wait!'

0014 MAN gazes up from bottom step and receives hurled blood into the nape of his neck.

Three Months After Implant Activation

001 SUBJECT and MAN order Hailo taxi to South Great George's.

002 Old Woman enquires if they can return with 'a white Magnum ice cream'.

003 SUBJECT says: 'Let's toss about in the breeze outside.'

004 MAN looks at shopfront of *Burrito Ville* when taxi halts.

005 'I'll take you for a nice bite to eat afterwards,' he tells SUBJECT.

006 SUBJECT sighs. 'Are you thinking of your stomach already?'

007 MAN acknowledges he has been 'drooling about black bean burritos' since SUBJECT informed him yesterday he had to accompany her to witness 'the excruciating pain of removal'.

008 'Christ, look, that bloody hipster with the firefly beard is still here sipping an Iced Chai Almond Milk Latte,' SUBJECT tells Man.

009 'Who?' MAN asks.

0010 'I told you about him, oh fuck it, never mind,' SUBJECT says. 'Point is he's looking at us like he knows we've been through the wars.'

0011 'By the looks of him I doubt he gives a fuck about anything,' MAN says.

0012 'Rock on,' third party says to MAN and SUBJECT prior to entering clinic.

0013 MAN smacks SUBJECT on bum going up stairs.

0014 'Stop it you bollix, I'm nervous,' SUBJECT explains.

0015 Receptionist charges MAN €150 on debit card.

0016 'He wants to know why you rip people off charging the same price as the original implant to remove this chemico piece of crap,' SUBJECT says.

0017 MAN responds: 'I never said that, I didn't say that.'

0018 'Look at him throwing a scalded look at me!' SUBJECT says, amused.

0019 'Now's your chance to ask them whatever happened the male pill?' SUBJECT says. 'This poor man hasn't had his end away in months, you'd feel for him, wouldn't you?'

0020 MAN walks off towards row of hard plastic chairs.

0021 Doctor exits from cubicle and says, 'No, not the man, he can't come in here, just you.'

0022: MAN showing visible signs of relief and takes out a copy of *Viz* comic.

0023 MAN assures SUBJECT he'll be 'right here' when she 'stumbles out'.

0024: MAN advises SUBJECT that 'he's going nowhere'.

0025 'Yes, I've always known that,' SUBJECT says.

0026 'This is going to hurt,' doctor informs SUBJECT.

0027 'Why did you do it?' SUBJECT asks MAN.

0028 'Now is not the time,' MAN replies.

0029 'Why did you fuck her?' SUBJECT asks MAN.

0030 'Now is not the time,' MAN repeats.

0031 'You can just see the future of abortion clinics in Ireland, can't you?' SUBJECT says to MAN.

0032 'What's that got to do with anything?' MAN says, seeming amused.

0033 'Me here, you there,' SUBJECT says, starting to cry. 'Why the fuck did I get this bastard thing into me in the first place?'

0034 'We'll have a nice meal afterwards,' MAN says.

0035 'Yeah, that'll do it,' SUBJECT says.

0034 Doctor closes door on MAN.

0036 Doctors informs SUBJECT implant is 'caught up in muscle tissue, requires hard pulling, with a stitch afterwards.'

0037 'We don't let men into the treatment rooms,' Doctor informs SUBJECT. 'They're just not able for what goes on in here.'

0038 SUBJECT says she 'understands how it goes'.

0039 'He fucked someone else and I blamed myself,' SUBJECT says.

0040 'I hear that a lot,' the Doctor remarks. 'You should look the other way for this.'

0041 'Yeah, I think I know how to do that,' SUBJECT informs Doctor.

ABORT ABORT ABORT ABORT ABORT ABORT
ABORT ABORT ABORT ABORT ABORT ABORT

Cadaverus Moves

There's a fan whirring and a smell of slag intestines snaking through to where I sit waiting to see a dead body for the first time. Yours, of course. And that *Remains of the Day* arsehole in full hat-tip regalia telling me it's a good idea to sip some water before I go in, like I might not even recognise you, uses the word 'Madam' from the Co-op Funeral Book, abbreviated 'Mme', plural Mesdames, who happen to be walking about outside smoking at the corrugated bins, talking about cheap cuts. You're fucking dead. Straight as a pea shoot. Let's get that out of the way from the getgo. Barley brushes of hell tickling the sky-chin of a giant torn tuna with a blood clot at the end of your nose for sucking brains through. White jelly shoes a gardener might like to stick small plants in to cheer someone up. Tumour mash scoops, mole hills, speed bumps, a face of sheer beaver. Wax hands, ten embedded wicks, historically used as a method of timekeeping and picking up flame-grilled chicken tits layered with Emmental cheese and back bacon, hickory-smoked BBQ sauce, seasoned fries and buttered peas. I walk outside. The roofs of Britain are pretty much the cardboard same. Piss ball up in the sky shining down on an awful lot of dogs and scratched cars. Those street drains small children throw cutlery into all summer. Seems pretty meaningless to me. So I suggest we go for a pint. It's the icing bar the two neon trannies from Blackpool own, where they bring other trannies for card games, dress-up nights and tin-can karaoke. The barman eyes you up pretty mean as if you've stolen the celebrity supplement of the Sunday paper, though he gets 'the look' back from me and serves us both to avoid some sort of face-off. You say nothing, gooing all around you, Mr Magoo, as if already, only twelve hours into rock-clot, you've forgotten the drama of being alive, the shit-arse boredom of it, the handing out of small change and tiny snatches of courteous dialogue in places like this that always have a launderette and enormous drive-in gizmo nearby with ATMs and small bags of rip-off coal. Ah sure, where would ye be going without a bell on yer bike? Better out than in. Like. If I don't see ye I'll see ye when I see ye. Phone calls have been made, sure, cos the door keeps beepin' 'n' creakin', a series of nods, string-boom of 'It can't be him!', followed by what I would call collective anger not felt since some skinny nurse of the war years sucked off a German soldier behind a plum tree in a public park and tried to keep it quiet. 'He'll have to go,' the barman says. 'Oh yeah, really?' I say, turning around to take them all on, one by one if needs be. 'Out!' he says. You were already gone, I was there. I could not have hated you more.

Etch A Sketch of a year since you were declared 'terminal'. I still ride the blanks and hope no one in the library notices. I set off most days with Arvo Pärt's *Spiegel im Spiegel* playing in my head. Out past the squiggle of purposeless shops and homeless men who nudge their heads up like broken birds from splintered eggs in the basement of the church. On to the Tolka Bridge where an orange city fox stalks me in the first draft of morning. Conversations become cataracts of sorts. 'Wouldn't it bite the toes right off ye?' a woman said at the bus stop last October when you rang with the news. 'I can't be doing with this heat!' the same woman stupidly says today in June. Time bungles by on the long borrow. You're still here, but fading. I pick you up at the airport and you're wearing a *Daily Mash* T-shirt with the words: DO NOT PANIC BUT YOU ARE GOING TO DIE. 'Funny as fuck!' you say, pushing the luggage trolley out into the main foyer. Your two teenage kids Hollie and Ryan hug me tight. Words eclipse. 'So this is it,' you say, scanning Arrivals. You are back in Ireland to say goodbye. A dance with neutrons and protons, that's what's ahead of you now. Sliding up and down wallpaper. Watching us in our daily drudge. You meet the women I work with. The building is Georgian, a carved wedding cake, crafted cornicing, walls of tedious green and piercing yellow. Corridors cropped in spiderweb wigs where the elderly shuffle through to read or snore or attend literary readings upstairs. Almost everyone who strolls in wears glasses and carries a spiked umbrella. There's a small café on the ground floor that serves tea, fair-trade coffee, tray bakes and ham sandwiches made at the curvature of dawn by an old crooked cook who reeks of rotten lilies. I feel proud showing you around. 'My brother, home from Ipswich.' You are only forty-seven, a dissolution. In the quiet clammy armpit of early afternoon we visit our parents. 'Be prepared,' I warn. 'He's pissing the house for ages, she's swimming in the Nile.' Our mother opens the door, gasps. I follow her into the kitchen. You head into the ogre in the sitting room. 'I got an awful land!' she says. 'Looks like someone shoved his head in an open fire.' Shakes uncontrollably. 'It's just the chemo, last batch was the hardest, proper burn.' I carry in a tray of tea and Kimberley biscuits. The kids chuckle on the couch. 'What's going on?' I ask. 'It's Grandad, we can't make out a word he's saying.' Happens a lot. Eighty-two, pickled brain. 'Have you still got a dickie tummy?' he asks. You take a deep breath. 'Cancer, I've explained several times on the phone, nothing they can do now.' Sneers. 'Rubbish!' he roars. 'A scam between the health insurance company and your job.' You run at him. 'No one pretends they're dying you mad bastard.' Grabbing his hand, you roll it around the bevy of tumours lumping out your gut like caddy fare. 'Can you feel them? They're real, you fucking moron.' You scour the house one last time, commenting on the size of the back garden, the freshly painted purple walls in the kitchen. 'I was going to use my share to buy a mobile home in France for holidays with the kids.' She gets weak. He stays in his chair. Kids' heads are lowered. I turned you into Workie the Lion, rode this hall on your back many times. Threw a wax apple at your head, alms of a scar. You gave me my first joint upstairs to the bawl of Bowie. 'Look after yourself,' she says. Final words. 'I love you, my sunshine.' Back at the flat I make your favourite monkfish curry but you push it away. 'Sorry, smells the dogs, just can't hold anything down.' We stroll out to the back garden. The night sky is clearer than I ever remember. Alabaster stars flickering against a plush overlay of navy. There it is as we crane our necks: a shooting star. A dying star. Zipping across the chaos on its way home. What a crummy beautiful coincidence. We clank our glasses and smile.

Knobby's high-rise flat in East London and there's a gun on the table. 'Man innit man innit' is all I can make out. Reggae tunes, loud and demanding. Too much Barney Rubble. Ain't it Mork and Mindy out. *Cunts cunts cunts.* One of his cronies wiping coke-snot from his hooter, rubbing runways of slick onto a gnarled hand. Fear ferreting up my legs so much I have to step out onto the balcony to glare at half-lit office blocks with tiny security men anting around inside. I'm shaking. Two other men wander in and out. Stare at my black velvet dress pulled over black tights tossed with white nylon spiders. We were meant to be celebrating other people's abortions. Trying to make fun of what's been hurting us. Some petite blonde from Dublin you were in love with, a gangster's wife. My ex-boyfriend who gave away my Morris Ital to a married woman who had a termination for him when we were still together. It is the summer of getting stoned, of taking risks. You wanted to score some blow. The pub we're drinking in earlier on this night is Pitbull rough, jammed with Stratford locals. Batches of bare tattooed arms and dreadlocks wall to wall. You are wearing a white shirt and a pink Irish fucked face, holding two flip bottles of Grolsch. Acid-house tunes persecuting the air. Long-legged women shimmying the carpet with slippy feet inside white sandals. You hand me a spliff to take outside. 'How do you do it?' you ask when I come back in. Do what? 'Fat one year, skinny the next.' Then you say, 'I have it sorted, we need to get into the car now.' You've had a welly of booze. We follow the Beamer to Knobby's flat. 'We'll take a lump and go if that's OK mate?' you say to Knobby. Not how it works around here. 'Nah, nah, you'll stay and have a toke, innit, get the lady a Vera Lynn.' One of the men pulls a chair up beside me, pushes in against my small thighs. 'You've a nice boat race,' he whispers. You tell him I'm your skin 'n' blister, to go easy. Knobby picks up the gun, shows it to you, peacock proud. 'This, my friend, is a fucking thing of high beauty.' The men laugh. One of them says. 'Not if you get it in the head, makes a right Elliot Ness.' The room spins. Voices mingle and merge until I'm no longer sure who's who, who I am, or you. The sitting room is brown. The men are brown. The night is brown. The pizza boxes are brown. The stash is brown. My eyes are yellow. 'No, no, that wouldn't be polite, c'mon now,' you say when they ask if they can have a go at me. I begin to sway. Bend forward, droop. My half-permed blonde hair serpent-tailing exposed shoulders. Someone's hand is on my arse. I wonder if this is it, if this is how we straggle to oblivion. I stop listening. Everything slows. It slows and I think how the years ahead may have been too fast for us to manage anyway. I wanted to go to university. I wanted to get my belly button pierced. I wanted to teach English in Japan. What if they rape you first? What if they fling me still breathing into a supermarket skip full of putrid fish and grey pork chops? What if they torture us, searing my legs with a house iron, slipping your eye out with a flick-knife? They ask if you'll deal for them. You politely decline. Silence slinks and slumps. I think of being a girl, shadowing strangers around the estate at dusk, eating snow off gritty walls. Your card gambling tin, all that dosh pinched by me for blue and orange sweets, Pink Panther chocolate bars. I think of drives to Glendalough, locked inside the navy Cortina with a small bottle of lemonade between four of us, legs stuck fast to the plastic seats in the back. I can't remember exactly why I left Ireland. You grab my elbow and say, 'Up, up, get up, thanks lads, keep it sweet.' Reef me out the door. We're in the piss graffiti lift with 'Mandy Is A Dirty Slag' on the ceiling. Me pressed up against the back panel mirror, hands slowly slipping down to my knees to balance myself, in tears. You, laughing, choking, spitting, yahooing. What year is it? Back out in the pitch-dark wet car park you say, 'Fuck me that was close, at least we have enough to do us till next week.' The wind batters my face from the rolled-down window. It is raining hard. You drive too fast. Our words slow to molasses.

I'm wearing a floppy wine corduroy hat, seersucker blouse, striped leggings, red boots, an awful lot of tiger's eye to ward off rich Jersey males who only tolerate whore's gold. 'It's weird here, they're into witchcraft as soon as the tourists go home.' You look midered, like you've just stepped out of a tube at Wood Green. Long silver trench coat, black shirt and trousers, silver winklepicker shoes. 'Caroline left a car for you, I think it's a Punto, she's too fucked most of the time to drive.' We take the coast road around the back of the island on into the Vic in the Valley where you immediately nab the pub manager's job and a small flat in a converted barn on the grounds. Twenty minutes on the island and you have transport, a job, a place to live. 'That's how you fucking do it, oh yeah baby!' you holler, rolling a joint on the dashboard. 'You have to be so careful here, they deport people for fuck all. It's illegal to dance on Sundays. All these strange laws. They out petty crime on the news every night at 6 p.m., even minor traffic offences. A Scottish builder was barred from the islands for stealing a garden gate. A Portuguese janitor got stuck inside a cow's vagina, found in a field the next day by police still clamped on. They photographed it for their files.' You stare out at the silver strips of sea and Elizabeth's Castle, grey and lumpy as an exotic elephant washing itself in a dust bath. 'Tell me about the Wizard,' you say. 'Your letters were so full of shit they almost made me piss myself.' I tell him, 'No, it's true, he's big into this Carlos Castaneda astral projection thing, travelling outside the body into other dimensions. His spirit guide is a soldier from the American Civil War.' You laugh so hard the car bonnet bashes bushes on the roadside. 'He says you can choose whether to be in this world or a dream world.' I want to tell you that I knew because one night after we'd taken tabs of acid, I got horny and stuck a roll-on deodorant bottle up me in bed. I don't know why I did it but they were all eating hummus on wheaten crackers downstairs, and the Wizard said to me, 'I could see what you were doing up there.' I stopped playing with myself after that and only bathed with a light nightdress on me. Caroline says it's all the sandalwood he burns, it's sent his brain somewhere else. I explain that you have to be Jersey-born and living on the island fifteen years before you're allowed rent somewhere with its own entrance or exit. Visitors like us can only get jobs in the service industry that supplies accommodation. 'How come you work in an office then?' you ask. I'm staying illegally in a luxury penthouse with a camembert-scoffing alcoholic who's the kept mistress of the Prince of Oman. 'She's not bullshiting either … he came one night with a flotilla of suited bodyguards to take her somewhere for posh fish.' I get £10 an hour for sticking labels on envelopes. It's £0.90 for twenty fags and £1.60 a pint. 'The locals out in the valley where you'll be speak a weird mixture of French and English that no one can understand.' You say, 'Fuck them.' My other friends live in a house on Le Geyt Street in the town centre with a jazz band, rented by the Wizard. 'You'll see for yourself, there's a man from Portsmouth who lies on the kitchen floor every night after downing a litre of vodka. He won the lotto, and lost his life.' No matter where you drive on the island eventually the capital, St Helier, sneaks into view. 'A lot of insurance companies,' you say. 'And banks. I'd say there's some rich fucks stashing their wedges of cash right here.' Hot as badgers, the last day of August. 'We go to a pizza place inside a cave at weekends. They put slices of raw garlic on the dough. Everyone eats Moules Marinières on a Sunday, it's the only full day workers get off. We get really messed up, you'll see for yourself.' We arrive at the house, Caroline jumps up to give you a hug. 'You're gas, look at you!' she says, amused by your formal attire. 'The jammy fucker got himself a job straight from the airport,' I tell her. The men in the house are all wearing shorts. She's going travelling around Thailand soon. 'Can I skin one up?' you ask, picking up a lump of yellow from the coffee table. 'Go easy on it,' I say. 'It's way stronger over here, comes straight in from Africa.' There's a man in the corner rubbing snails on his face from inside the patio door, he thinks they're ice cubes. Geraldine is out in the yard rubbing vanilla ice cream on her legs to cool herself down. The Wizard introduces his girlfriend Theresa and says she's a reincarnated town crier. He tells you that the apocalypse happened thousands of years ago and genial aliens came from an outer galaxy to build the pyramids and help us start up again. 'Nice one,' you say. 'And I hear you drive a bin truck during the day, how does that work for you?' Caroline laughs. Nine cats with the same life stroll about mewing for meat in the vegetarian kitchen that's growing its own bean sprouts in the tile grouting. We get totally fucked and end up lying on the parquet floor. 'I think I'm going to enjoy this gig,' you say. Later into the night when everyone is slumped open-mouthed on damask chairs, you steal the Wizard's girlfriend. Riding her hard in the spare room upstairs until she calls you 'daddy' and asks for more. Hippy hell breaks loose. You never get to see the jazz band play. The Wizard puts a curse on you. 'I'll get E.T. to do him up the arse next time he's in town,' you say.

There's an oil-slick all along the beach in Blackpool when we get our first proper look at the promenade. Blackened seagulls and other smaller birds stiff in horror, a forfeit of high commerce. 'Isn't that terrible, I bet there'll be no swimsuit competition this year,' our mum says. We look at each other and snicker. Moonhead is pissed out of his balls driving the car. He forbids any more 'children's talk' until he can get another double whiskey down the gullet. But we are too excited. 'Look at the trams!' I say. 'Big deal,' you say. 'Shut it,' Mum says. 'Yeah, shut it,' Moonface says. At the Sunnybank B&B a Welsh woman with huge tits and plaited loaves high hair tells us the oil slick has caused a lot of damage to business. 'The husband's a pansy,' Moonhead says, as we make our way up the stairs. 'They said they keep the resident's bar open until 1 a.m.' There are two single beds and a double in the room, a shower and toilet shared with another couple from the Isle of Man. Dinner is served in small silver bowls: hot chicken soup with reconstituted small vegetables floating around, followed by chicken and chips, and strawberry ice cream served in the same silver bowls, still warm from the soup. 'All the way from Ireland,' the Welsh woman says, pointing us out to the other diners who stare and nod. 'I put plastic dog shit in his bed,' you say, knowing that Moonface was born minus a sense of humour and will punch one of us in the face for misbehaving. 'Don't!' I plead. 'Just don't.' Every holiday in Blackpool starts the same way. 'We're going to the Tower Ballroom tonight, your father wants a dance, and tomorrow we'll hit the Pleasure Beach,' Mum says, looking stupidly happy. 'I'm going to a punk disco,' you announce. 'I saw a poster for it earlier.' Mum says, 'On your nelly, you're only thirteen.' Outside the streets are flushed with red and blue windmills, buckets and spades, giant jelly infant soothers, 'Kiss Me Quick' felt bowler hats, polystyrene triangles loaded with smelly periwinkles. I try skipping along but you keep pushing me into small bumpy walls, scraping the skin on my arms. There are donkeys being pulled home along the pathways by vendors. Candy floss lights up fairy pink under flashing neon on makeshift fairground stalls. Bingo men shout out numbers. Face painters pull us in and Moonface pulls us out again. Inside the Tower there's a map of what's on each floor: an aquarium, Jungle Jim's, a soft-ball pit, a dungeon, a circus. We're herded into the lift to the darkened dance hall and told to 'sit still' while they hit the floor. 'I'm off,' you say. 'Tell them I've gone to the toilet.' I wait around for a while and go look for you. You're kissing a girl called Paula at a viewing window three floors above. It is a shock to see you kissing someone but you seem to know how to do it proper.

'Piss off,' you say. You're getting too grown up for me. Moonface is seething we left the drinks unattended at their table. Some gobshite has taken away a globule of yellow that was still sat happy in his glass. 'Where's that pup?' he asks about you, but I will not tell, not now or into forever. A bald man bangs an organ and Mum says, 'Isn't this lovely, aren't we having a great time!' A security man pulls you into the ballroom, dragging you towards mum and Moonface. 'Is he yours?' he asks, as if you are a dog. 'He's been drinking beer out there in the corridor.' This is a terrible thing to happen. Moonface says, 'You'll get my belt later.' You look away and don't seem to care. All the way back Mum is saying, 'Don't, for God's sake they're on their holidays.' At the B&B Moonface slams the front door, unable to contain his anger. Mum says, 'Go upstairs, I'll take your father to the bar to calm him down.' You jump on the bed and tell me you got the tit off Paula and are meeting her tomorrow night for more. I don't know what this means but I can tell you are excited. 'Do you love her?' I ask and you say you might well do, for a week anyway. 'Look!' you shout, with your head full out the window, legs splayed behind. 'It's unreal.' I run over and stick my head out. 'What? Where?' I say. You pull the heavy Victorian window down onto the small of my back, jamming me into place. 'Tell them I've gone to the punk disco, I'm a teenager now, I can do what the fuck I like.'

You're an egg-throwing mop of blonde. A fire toting Wild Indian of six burning fire spitting fire room to room. No one can stop you. A mother tries a sister tries two brothers try. Run screaming from room to room across the imprint of lino squares, kitchen press twine in your hair, hand smacking your mouth to make the screams even louder, bursting out in bags of air, breaking small toys under wildcatting feet, hands spinning knocking anything over in your fireball of go sending newspapers weather balloon upwards, stories of guerrilla warfare in other countries far away in mid 1970. Out to the front garden to the piercing light to the horny dogs barking to the sandy-coloured Labrador dogs that tear back in through the gloss silver gates after you and run in circles kicking up muck so excited around the carefully planted line of rose bushes. Roses of yellow with tea fragrance and delicious fruity undertones, red roses that smell of bagatelle nothing but make great hammocks for fat whirring bees. Spinning circles of children and happy animals, of thrown down tennis rackets and abandoned footballs rolling with the wind into the centre where the grass is thickest and flattened by rusty bicycles and doll prams. All the other children on the street are screaming Wild Indian too. Scorching surging citron rays of summer. Brown tights on small faces pulled from underwear drawers when someone big and bulky in a pinafore is at work out the back pushing wet clothes through a hand-operated roller, pungent smells of vegetable patch manure on tall rhubarb. They hear you screaming and join in, belting in from other gardens, hands grabbing hands falling rolling legs in blue shorts, rolling right up to the grey bumpy nodules of half walls bashing each other, bruised knees with patches of green. Aulones with croissant-curls shove their heads out white iron windows to say 'whissst' and 'stop that' and 'there'll be wigs on the green if you keep this up!' You gather your posse and tear through the house out into the back garden up onto the coal shed over onto the garage jumping down onto the wall in the front garden and back in circles to do it all over again. 'Stop this!' our mother roars. 'Jesus Christ, I'm gone half mad.' She snatches you by the scruff and closes the front door on the other kids without explanation. 'Get in there and calm the hell down, I didn't ask for a bluebottle for a son.' I am splayed on the couch in a cloth nappy, my legs flailing. 'You are a slug,' you tell me and I laugh. My big wide eyes follow you left/right/left/right as you run around the couch screaming 'peekaboo peekaboo', falling to your knees if front of me so I can just see your head. 'When you little missy came along I poured Ma's perfume down the sink and flushed her wedding ring down the jacks.' I gurgle and swing my arms at you but they can't reach. My knees are cold, milky spit dribbles from my mouth. 'I was going to throw you down the stairs to break your neck. Then I started to like you even if you smell.' You jump up and run around the couch in the opposite direction screaming 'peekaboo peekaboo' until you run out of wind. 'You might not know this yet because you're so stupid and small, but I was here before you and I'll always be Ma's favourite.' I laugh uncontrollably as you are just unbelievably great. 'I am your very big handsome brother,' you say. 'I'm taller than you and better than you and cleverer than you and more special than you, but I am still your big brother.' You start to twist on the ground, gripping your knees tight as you go, spinning like a tomato, howling out the words I will always be so happy to hear: 'I am your brother, I am your brother, I am your brother.'